PUFFIN BOOKS

THE BROKEN SADDLE

Eric, the poorest boy in a small Australian town, doesn't seem to have a real life of his own. Whether at school or on the street, he's always on the outside of what's going on. Somehow other people's lives just seem more important. Until one Saturday, in one of his fleeting visits home, Eric's drover father gives him a pony and Eric's life changes dramatically overnight.

Riding gives Eric more contact with other people and when he is befriended by one of the richest men in the town he suddenly finds that he has to make some important decisions.

This is a startlingly different story about a powerful relationship between a boy and his horse. Provocative and compelling, its totally unexpected ending will leave you wondering for a long time to come.

JAMES ALDRIDGE

The Broken Saddle

PUFFIN BOOKS

Puffin Books, Penguin Books Ltd, Harmondsworth, Middlesex, England
Viking Penguin Inc., 40 West 23rd Street, New York, New York 10010, U.S.A.
Penguin Books Australia Ltd, Ringwood, Victoria, Australia
Penguin Books Canada Ltd, 2801 John Street, Markham, Ontario, Canada L 3 R 1 B 4
Penguin Books (N.Z.) Ltd, 182 190 Wairau Road, Auckland 10, New Zealand

—

First published in Great Britain by Julia MacRae Books 1983
Published in Puffin Books 1984

—

Copyright © James Aldridge, 1982
All rights reserved

—

Made and printed in Great Britain
by Richard Clay (The Chaucer Press)
Bungay, Suffolk
Set in Monophoto Ehrhardt by
Northumberland Press Ltd, Gateshead, Tyne and Wear

Chapter 1

Mrs Thompson lived in one of the oldest houses in the town of St Helen, and some said it was already there when the explorers Burke and Wills forded the river at St Helen on their journey across Australia from south to north, which they never completed because they died of starvation half-way. But that was sixty or seventy years ago, and though the town now had cars, paved streets, a row of shops, three schools, stock-yards, banks, and even two small private aeroplanes, the old house looked as if it had been built and left there by the early pioneers. It was very low and very small, and it was sheltered by wide verandahs in front as well as at the back. The front garden was simply a sandy patch, except for a large mound about ten feet square thick with violets, which you could smell a block away when the violets were in bloom. Otherwise the violet bed smelled of the horse manure which Mrs Thompson used to keep the violets young and lovely.

In fact Mrs Thompson looked a little like the house. She was not old, but she was tiny and sunburnt and good-natured and shy, as if she were always sheltering from something. And her son, Eric, was like his mother – a small, quicksilver boy with snow-white hair, green eyes, bare feet, and as good-natured as his mother though intensely curious, so that everything in the town seemed ready and waiting for his personal inspection, which was often quickly in and as quickly out.

It was the time of the great depression in Australia when there was plenty of poverty, even in small country towns like

St Helen, and the Thompsons were one of the poorest families in the town. Their house was more or less bare, except for a clothes cupboard, a kitchen table with four chairs, a big wooden trunk, two beds and, outside on the verandah, a wash stand near a water tap. It was often said in the town that the Thompsons possessed so little that it was safe to say that they possessed nothing at all.

Mr Thompson was a drover, and Eric and Mrs Thompson rarely saw him because he was mostly following cattle or sheep a thousand miles away. Sometimes he sent money home and sometimes he did not. Mostly he did not because he seemed to forget them for long periods at a time so that Mrs Thompson had to work to keep herself and Eric in food and clothes – what little they had of both. Mrs Thompson sewed up dresses and curtains, repaired sheets and cooked jams and conserves for other people in their kitchens. She washed the walls of the small private hospital once a month, and when anybody was sick and needed help in the house she was sometimes sent for to work around the house, cooking and cleaning, which she did as long as she was needed or as long as she was paid. Often, people forgot to pay her, but she would go on working anyway and never ask for her money, until Eric would have to come and stand, one bare foot on the other, and ask for it.

Eric's life as a boy could be divided into two stages: before Saturday, December 2, and after it, because that particular Saturday would change his life, although it was a little more complicated than that.

The trouble with Eric was that he wanted to be friendly with everyone, and he went out of his way to greet almost everyone in town – man, boy, girl and any passing animals as if, in offering his own friendship, he could find friends of his own. But it never worked out that way. He knew almost everybody in the town, and on his way to and from school, or going anywhere at all, he would shout a greeting to Mr

Jackson, or to Mr Phillips, or to Bob the milkman or Jack Scott the mechanic.

'Hello, Jack,' he would call as Jack went by in his Willys car.

If Jack had seen him he would wave a casual, greasy hand. If not, then Eric's greeting simply disappeared in the dust swirl of the old car that Jack kept together by his genius as a mechanic.

Most people greeted Eric and were friendly, though usually brief. If he passed Mrs Halford in her garden he would say, 'Hello, Mrs Halford' and stand at the fence for a moment, one bare foot on the other.

Mrs Halford usually looked up at Eric's smiling face and said,

'Oh hello Eric. How is your mother?'

'All right thanks,' he would reply and stand for a moment as if expecting the conversation to go on. But Mrs Halford always went back to her gardening and after a moment Eric would say, 'Goodbye, Mrs Halford,' and if she thought about it she might say goodbye. Or, if she was too busy, she wouldn't bother to reply but would simply wave her hand.

Yet it was Mrs Halford who understood Eric's problem. She said to her son, Bob, who was a little older than Eric but clever like his mother, 'Why don't you make friends with young Eric Thompson?'

Bob thought about it for a moment and said, 'Because he's always trying to make friends with me.'

'What's the matter with that?' his mother asked.

'I don't know,' Bob said to her. 'Snow's all right. But he's always too friendly. He wants to be friends with everybody, and that's no good if you want to have a friend of your own. That's his trouble.'

'Don't you like him?'

'He's all right,' Bob said again with an Australian shrug, 'but why doesn't he stick to himself sometimes?'

Mrs Halford, who knew and liked Mrs Thompson, said: 'The Thompsons are poor people, and poor people never know what to do to forget it. I can tell you this, Bob: you'll never be invited into that little house for a meal or a glass of lemonade because they know that most people are embarrassed by their poverty. So the Thompsons are always protecting themselves somehow, both Eric and his mother.'

'They've got a funny way of doing it,' Bob said. 'Anyway, why is he always smiling if he's so poor?'

'Because that's about all he's got to offer the world,' Mrs Halford said and forgot the Thompsons, which most people usually did after a few moments' concern.

So Eric went on greeting everybody, and whenever he could he would join any group that formed at school or on the street. He seemed always to be there; but inevitably, in whatever game or close-knit cabal other boys were involved with, sooner or later he would be left out, and nobody noticed when he disappeared. He didn't seem to mind. Moreover he knew almost every place in town where he could watch men at work, as if in watching he became part of the casual companionship of men doing things.

At the Chrysler garage where Jack Scott worked, Eric knew how to appear quietly in the big corrugated-iron shed at the back where local Chryslers were repaired, and he would squat near the pit where Jack was working and say: 'Hello Jack. Is that Mr Peters' car?'

'That's right,' Jack would say, and get on with his grunting and pushing and swearing as he worked on some difficult nut.

If Jack occasionally asked Eric to pass him a spanner or a piece of dirty rag or a tin for the sump oil, Eric had it done almost before the thing was asked for.

'Thanks, Snow...' Jack would say and this time Eric would say nothing but wait for some new request, which rarely came. It almost always ended by Jack saying, 'You'd

8

better hop it now. No use hanging around here getting your feet dirty.' And Jack would laugh at his own joke.

'See you tomorrow,' Eric would call over his shoulder as he disappeared.

He liked to watch the type-setter who produced the lead slugs of type for the local paper. Suddenly Bill Phillips would be aware of two bare feet behind him as his fingers raced lightly over the keys; but this was one place where Eric knew that he had to speak only when he was spoken to, because Mr Phillips could make a mistake if he was surprised by a greeting or a question.

'How did you get in here?' he would usually say to Eric.

'The back way,' Eric would reply.

'Then you'd better get out the back way,' Mr Phillips would tell him.

But Eric knew he was not unfriendly and he would stand, as usual, waiting for more conversation. When it didn't come he made his own.

'Could you spare a couple of lead slugs for fishing sinkers, Mr Phillips?' he asked.

Mr Phillips pointed to a kerosene tin near his linotype which had some rejected lines of lead in it. 'Take two,' he said, 'and then scat.'

Eric took two of the shiny metal slugs and was over the back fence and away before Mr Phillips was back at work with his nimble, trembling fingers.

Eric knew who owned every bike, car, horse, buggy, truck and motorcycle in town. He watched Mr Caldwell, who drove the Shell petrol lorry, filling up the underground tanks outside Smith's garage.

'Don't hang around here, Snow,' Mr Caldwell told him. 'If this thing blows up your mother won't know you from a speck of dust.'

This time Eric laughed and left Mr Caldwell to his dangerous job.

He would appear sometimes at the butter factory where Pat Radford sat at a table near the big churn taking butter out of the large rotating wooden barrel. She would then cut the lump of yellow butter into rectangular little blocks with wooden pats, slapping each block into squares and then half wrapping it and weighing it and adding an ounce or two – all so speedily done that Eric would watch it for hours without boredom. But when Pat saw him there she always asked the same question:

'Did you wipe your feet, Eric?'

The tiled floor was always slightly damp, and the whole place was so cool and clean that Eric would always wipe his feet very carefully on the damp cloth over the back door-step.

'You bet,' Eric said.

'Do you want to buy some butter?' Pat asked as she continued to slap the butter with the wooden pats.

'No, I just wanted to watch.'

'Well, don't let Mr Lewis catch you,' she said.

Mr Lewis owned the butter factory and he was one of the few people in the town who aimed a kick or a cuff at Eric, although he had no intention of actually landing the blow.

'You dirty young rascal,' he would shout. 'Keep out of my factory.'

'Okay Mr Lewis,' Eric would say as he ducked and ran. But he always came back because he knew that Mr Lewis's bark was worse than his bite.

A normal day in Eric's life covered, after school, any one or more of these visits and observations. He watched mail being loaded into vans at the Post Office, he inspected the railway trucks being loaded with dried fruit, wheat, oranges, or unloaded with tractors or harvesters. He knew the back of every shop, the fire station, the Co-op timber yard, the cattle yard. Men standing outside a pub, chatting, would sometimes find him standing close by listening, and if one of them was a little drunk, Eric would either be sent packing or given a sixpence and a friendly cuff from someone who would say: 'It's Andy Thompson's kid.'

In all this brief but continuing activity there were, in fact, only two people in the town whom he counted on as personal friends, but because of what they were they didn't really count as such. One of them was Father O'Connel, the Catholic priest, who always stopped to talk to Eric.

'Hello, Eric old son,' he would say. 'What are you up to now? No good I'll be bound.' The priest's smile was broad and his slap on Eric's back was a personal gesture.

'No. I'm not doing anything,' Eric would reply. 'Honest.'

'You're always up to something, so it's no use trying to fool me.'

'I was just going down to Mr Jackman's to watch him climb the telegraph pole behind the Post Office.'

'A likely story.'

Eric was always aware that Father O'Connel was having an elaborate game with him, and he was in no hurry to bring it to an end. Yet, feeling rather guilty, it was Eric who sometimes cut it short, although he didn't quite know why. Eric was not a Catholic and that was significant in this town which was divided into Catholics and Protestants. So, much as he appreciated Father O'Connel, Eric knew that the difficulties of age and religion and his own inability to play the little game for long, made of Father O'Connel the one man he always liked to talk to, but couldn't really do so freely.

The other friend who was not quite a friend but who was his own age had the most obvious of all limitations because she was a girl. Moreover she was the daughter of one of the richest men in the town. Dora Hunt's father not only owned the biggest grocery store in St Helen but he owned four or five other stores in neighbouring townships. Mr Hunt was an ardent, amateur horseman and kept two riding horses for himself and his wife. But he was always generous with his greetings to Eric.

'Eric, or little by little,' he would call out to Eric sometimes from his Dodge, and then he would laugh. So would Eric, although he never quite knew what Mr Hunt meant.

But Dora Hunt, for some reason that Eric never quite understood, liked him and was willing to talk to him, even though he was probably the poorest and worst-dressed boy in the town.

'What's it like living in that tiny little house?' she once asked Eric.

'What do you mean?' he said.

'I mean, it must be like living in a doll's house.'

'No, it isn't,' Eric said with a rare need to defend his house and home. 'It's the same as living in your house.'

'I suppose it is,' Dora said, 'but I'd love to see in it sometimes.'

Eric didn't offer to show it to her, because he knew without needing to know that nobody would ever be invited into his house.

'I like your mother,' Dora told him.

In fact Mrs Thompson liked Dora and so did Eric, but apart from their brief and welcome conversations Eric knew the complications that limited what he and Dora could say to each other, or do together.

'Goodbye Eric,' Dora would say as Eric broke it off after a surreptitious and admiring inspection of Dora's neat dress, shiny shoes, plaited hair.

'S'long,' Eric said, reluctant to add her name, but nonetheless secretly considering Dora Hunt his best, probably his only real-friend-non-friend.

Thus another day would pass and at night he would tell his mother what he had done, who he had seen, what he had heard; and Mrs Thompson was as interested as Eric was. 'What did Pat do?' she would ask. 'What did Mr Phillips say?' And, 'Was Dora neat the way she always is? I don't know how she keeps her hair so clean.' And from time to time she would say, 'And what happened then?' Afterwards, Eric would also hear from his mother what she had done and heard. But it was rare that mother or son reported what they themselves had said, as if that was not important, even between themselves.

Like that, they lived their life in their own way, which never altered because there was nothing in sight to alter it, until that Saturday, December 2, when something did come in sight, very much so; doubly so; and Eric's life changed quite dramatically overnight.

Chapter 2

Saturday, December 2, began like any normal Saturday. Eric had three ways of making a little money and they were all Saturday jobs. At five o'clock every Saturday morning he would arrive at the house of Councillor Sansom – a large old house on the main street surrounded by a mixed orchard of fifty orange trees, dozens of peach and apricot trees, and a variety of other fruit, all of which needed water. And early morning was the time to deliver it. Mr Sansom himself couldn't do it because he owned two farms and a vineyard at Nooah and he was seldom at home, so his wife had to organize the garden.

Eric's task was to turn on two taps at opposite ends of the big garden and keep the water flowing in the complex pattern of little irrigation channels that led from one tree to another. But before he reached the taps he had to pacify Patch, Councillor Sansom's Alsatian dog who barked at any stranger inside or outside the long picket fence. Eric was as friendly to dogs, cats, horses and cows as he was to human beings, and whenever he walked past the Sansoms' picket fence he would talk to Patch, so that eventually Patch, though still barking fiercely, changed his tone to a greeting rather than a threat. Nonetheless Patch had to use his threatening bark to anyone arriving at five in the morning, and Eric had to spend a few minutes changing it to a welcome, and finally to silence.

Like the people in the town, once he had made his position clear Patch simply walked away, and Eric was never able to pat him. But on this Saturday, as if it were auspicious of later events, Patch came close enough to sniff at Eric's bare legs, look him straight in the eye, and accept a light stroke from a couple of fingers before turning away and taking up his usual position under a pomegranate bush at the end of the fence.

'Well I'll be damned,' Eric said, as he watched him go.

Eric did his duty with the taps, using a hoe to block one canal or the other, guided the water around each tree, and when he had finished at seven o'clock he stood at the wire screen door at the back of the house until Mrs Sansom, who always wore a man's hat, interrupted her breakfast of chops, eggs and fried potatoes.

'Did you do all the trees, Eric?' she demanded.

'The lot, Mrs Sansom,' Eric said.

'You didn't miss the apricots?'

'No. I did them after the peaches.'

'You turned the taps off tight?'

'As tight as I could, but they both drip.'

'That's good for the mint,' Mrs Sansom said and, opening her right hand, she gave Eric a hot, damp, two-shilling piece. 'Now take that straight home,' she said to him. 'D'you hear?'

'Don't worry,' Eric said, wondering why he had to be told something he would do anyway. Saturday money went straight home to his mother: what else was he going to do with it, since he knew that she counted on it as a necessity.

His second task was to sit at a meat-sodden table in a little room behind Mr MacAllister's butcher shop and straighten out and sort out according to size the old newspapers that Mr MacAllister wrapped his meat in. Mr MacAllister was the smallest and cheapest butcher in town, and he did everything himself, because his wife was dead and his only son had run away years ago, taking the shop's bicycle with him.

Eric was one of the few people that Mr MacAllister actually spoke to first, because most of the time when he had to deal with customers he only replied to them, although when he did reply it was always friendly. His silent question of a customer:

'*What would you like?*' was asked by raised eyebrows and a slight cock of his head. His confirmation of an order was a very thoughtful nod, as if a pound of chump chops needed very serious consideration.

But to Eric he would always volunteer a statement, as he did today, as if his instructions needed speech. 'Sort that lot out, Eric,' he said, pointing to a rather grubby pile of newspapers in a corner. 'Make sure you throw away the jammy ones and the bloody ones. They cause a lot of trouble.'

In unfolding the newspapers, which Mr MacAllister bought for a penny a pound from boys who collected them, and in sorting them out according to their size (the big ones were *The Age Argos* from Melbourne as well as the local *Sentinel*, and the small one was the *Melbourne Sun*) Eric often found not only jam stuck to the middle sheets, but a variety of other stains: tomato sauce, grease, food particles, beer rings, tea and sometimes blood from previous wrappings.

'Don't worry,' Eric said. 'I'll sort them out, Mr Mac-Allister.' Eric waited, as usual, for more talk, even though he knew quite well that nothing would come. 'They look pretty dirty,' he added.

Mr MacAllister nodded and re-nodded as if a serious business had been settled, and he left Eric to his work. Eric spread the papers out flat and slit the folds with a blunt butcher's knife so that they would all be ready for Mr Mac-Allister to slap the meat on the top page and bundle it up in one sheet not two. It was all a matter of economics because Mr MacAllister was the poor man's butcher. He was not very well off himself, and Eric knew instinctively that his job for a shilling a week was not really for Mr MacAllister but was something that Mr MacAllister did for his mother. Mr MacAllister sometimes added a pound of mutton chops as a bonus for 'a neat job, Eric'.

Half-way through the sorting and cutting Eric was visited by Lilac, Mr MacAllister's cat, who was called Lilac because she had almost violet eyes. She leapt up on the table and sat on the pile of papers and inspected Eric who said, 'Hello Lilac, get off!' though he didn't mean it. In fact Lilac tolerated a few strokes down her back, vibrated her tail, and leapt down. Being a cat in a shop full of free meat, Lilac refused to touch any of it. She lived on milk and oatmeal porridge, which cost money.

'Mouse, Lilac!' Eric tried on her, leaping up in mock urgency. 'Over there.'

Lilac knew better, and licked her right paw. And, watching her, Eric knew that there was something about this cat that he didn't like. Or rather he came to an unusual and forceful conclusion.

'I'd hate to be a cat.'

In fact he liked Lilac, but he had to make his preference for ordinary human contact by declaring himself the antithesis of the cat.

When he left Mr MacAllister he was given a shilling and a bundle of sausages with a quick, important nod, which was Mr MacAllister's normal thank you.

Before his third and last job, which Eric enjoyed most, he went home for his breakfast of fried bread, jam and tea, and in reporting his brief friendship with Patch, the dog, Mrs Thompson said, as she had many times before:

'The last time that dog got out in the street he tore the leg off Mr Wakeford's trousers. He was just riding his bike along the street and Patch attacked him, and he spilled all his letters all over the place.'

Mr Wakeford was the postman and it was Eric's turn to say, 'Mr Wakeford told Councillor Sansom that the next time Patch attacked him he'd shoot him.'

'He'd never do that . . .'

They went on exchanging news and old information so that life seemed to be fixed and unchanging and, despite Mrs Thompson's endless and secret and worrying financial (and other) difficulties, they seemed secure in their mutual dependence.

Eric's third job was at Mr Hunt's (Dora's father) grocery store; in the big storage room at the back. But he was not going there to work for Mr Hunt, he was really employed by 'Slash' Jameson. Nobody seemed to remember how Slash got his name, but like many Australian nicknames it was an opposite, because Slash was a neat, precise, proud, professional grocer's assistant of nineteen, who had never slashed anything in his life except perhaps a piece of cheese, and even that he cut expertly and beautifully with a pull wire. Though Slash was the junior among the three grocery employees, he already had the confidence and conviction that here was his life, and his successful and happy future in it was only a matter of time. Someday he would either manage Mr Hunt's store, or end up having his own. Every morning, when he wrapped his ankle-length white apron around his waist and attached it at the back with a polished brass hook with a heart at the other end, he was setting about organizing and packaging the needs of a community as expertly and efficiently as possible.

Being the junior, Slash was supposed to build up a ready-packed store of weighed and bagged potatoes in seven, fourteen and twenty-one pound bags, but Slash considered potato-weighing beneath his true grocer's dignity. So he paid two shillings a week out of his hard-earned money for Eric to do the job for him. Mr Hunt was a liberal employer, and while considering Slash a little bit mad, he didn't object so long as the potatoes were weighed accurately, and the bags closed properly.

Eric was about to open a large sack of potatoes near the big black scales when he saw Dora Hunt's polished black shoes near him.

'Dad says you're the best potato weigher he's ever had,' Dora said, teasing him a little as he looked up at her.

In fact it was true, because Eric took his time and made

sure that each bag contained the exact weight, not an ounce more or less.

'I'm really doing it for Slash,' Eric told her.

'I know,' she said, and went on, 'Why doesn't Slash do it himself?'

'I dunno,' Eric said. 'I suppose he's too busy.'

'No, he isn't,' Dora said. 'Dad says he doesn't like getting his hands or his apron dirty.'

'Well, he has to keep clean,' Eric pointed out.

That was a point. By the time Eric had finished weighing the potatoes he would be covered in potato dust from his snow-white hair to his bare legs and feet.

'Do you want me to get you a piece of broken chocolate?' Dora asked him.

Dora was a favourite with everybody in her father's shop, and she could take anything she wanted from the shelves. But she rarely took advantage of it, particularly at the sweets counter. A piece of broken chocolate from the jar was, for some reason or another, more desirable than the perfect thing.

Eric nodded as he concentrated on his weighing, and when Dora returned with the chocolate he ate it with his dirty fingers and without any idea of taking it home. He knew without thinking about it that some things were his own, and it would please his mother as much as it pleased him to report this sudden bounty.

'See you Monday,' Dora said as she left.

'Taroo,' Eric said and looked for a tiny potato to bring a seven pound bag up to the exact weight.

When Eric had finished this chore, Slash flipped him his two-shilling piece, as if he wanted no physical contact at all with the potatoes or their weigher. And that was the normal part of Saturday, December 2, over and done with, except for Eric's quick, lightning look into the diesel power station, the blacksmith's, and his first swim of the summer in the river, so that by the time he reached home at five o'clock, Saturday was almost over and it was only when he was sitting down to tea with his mother at six o'clock, eating Mr MacAllister's sausages, that both of them were startled to hear a voice outside shouting,

'Maggie . . .'

Eric saw his mother's eyes open wide, and then she brought her two hands up to her face. It took her a long time to say something.

'It's him,' she whispered. 'It's your father.'

She didn't move, and Eric didn't know what to do. At the moment he could hardly remember his father, whom he had last seen a year ago when he had gone off with two other drovers in a buggy, trailing three horses. He remembered his mother crying quietly to herself that night when she thought he was asleep, and also counting the money which she kept in a tin in the floor under her bed. The next day she had given him a pair of old and worn shoes belonging to his father and told Eric to drop them in the river, a gesture of protest rare in his mother. She had said to him: 'And make sure they sink.'

'Maggie . . .'

'All right, Andy,' Mrs Thompson said now, and telling Eric to stay still she hurried outside. By now Eric too was wide-eyed, and he sat still at the kitchen table listening to his father and mother outside.

'Didn't you hear me?' Andy Thompson was saying, and hearing his voice Eric began to remember his father as a tall, morose man, with eyes that didn't seem to see anything because they didn't want to see anything.

'I didn't realize it was you,' Mrs Thompson was saying.

'Is there somebody else in this town who calls you Maggie?' Andy said to her.

'I don't know, Andy. I just wasn't thinking.'

Eric heard his father cough and spit, and then say something he didn't understand. Then his father came through the wire door to the back verandah and said to Mrs Thompson, 'I'll wash up a bit and then I'll have some tea.'

When Mrs Thompson came into the kitchen ahead of Andy she looked at Eric as if she didn't know what to do or say, so Eric sat still and waited as he knew how to wait, until his father came in. He expected a tall, thin man who would be about the same age as his mother. Instead he was startled to see that his father was an old man, and rather than thin he was lank and dry and leathery and worn, and his face was so sunburnt that Eric could hardly see any feature at all in it except the bright green eyes he had inherited himself. And here his other memory was correct: his father's eyes seemed to look without seeing anything, even though he was inspecting Eric closely.

'You haven't grown much,' he said to Eric.

'Hello, Dad,' Eric said, smiling at his father the way he smiled at everybody.

His father sat down opposite Eric as if this was what he did every day of the week. While he waited for his wife to give him food he said nothing to Eric, as if silence too had to be unseeing. Talk was only talk when it was necessary.

'The kelpie's outside, and he'll need some scraps,' Andy said to Mrs Thompson.

'I haven't got any scraps,' Mrs Thompson replied as she fried the last two sausages. 'I wasn't expecting you.'

'Haven't you got a bit of mutton on the bone?'

'I haven't got a thing. I didn't expect you, Andy.'

Andy seemed to give the situation a moment of grim but careful thought. Then he looked at Eric with his unseeing eyes and said, 'Have you finished your tea?'

'Yes, Dad,' Eric said.

'Have you got a bike?'

Eric was so startled by the suggestion, particularly from his father, that he laughed and said idiotically, 'Who? Me?'

'That's right.'

'No, not me,' Eric said.

'Eric, you go outside now,' his mother ordered, and though it was rare that she spoke to him like that, he recognized an appeal in her voice.

'All right,' he said.

'Just a moment. I want you to do something for me,' his father said as Eric got up to go. And though he knew that his mother wanted him to get out of the way quick, he was afraid to move, and curious too. What could his father want of him?

'Do you know where the stockyards are?'

'Of course,' Eric said as boldly as he could.

'Then you can run down there and you'll see Bob and Perce with the buggy and my tack. You ask them for my clothes bag, and ask them for a bit of meat for the kelpie.'

By now Mrs Thompson had managed to find some courage of her own, and she said, 'Why didn't you bring your things with you? The stockyard is over a mile away.'

'I came ahead in Joe Richards' Dodge,' Mr Thompson said in his old and long-distance sort of voice. 'Off you go,' he said sharply to Eric, ignoring his wife's protest.

As Eric went out he glanced unhappily for a moment at both his mother and father, and much later in his life he would come to realize that his father had spent a lifetime, even from childhood, living behind sheep or cattle, and that some time in the latter part of his life he had married a young woman and tried to settle down in St Helen. But the plan had soon failed, despite the birth of a son. One day Andy had packed up and simply gone back to the only life he could live: the silent, endless, drift behind the tails of animals, so that his contact with the wife and son he saw so rarely was as unseeing as the bright green eyes that were spoiled by the vast Australian distance. He saw nothing because he had spent a lifetime looking at nothing. In the end it was inevitable that he should forget them most of the time.

Outside, Eric almost tripped over the kelpie. He was lying

near the step, head flat to the ground like any good sheep or cattle dog.

'Hello, kelpie,' Eric said happily and sat down near him to rub his ears and nose. The kelpie accepted it, soft-eyed, but didn't move.

'Dad,' Eric called out. 'Can I take the kelpie with me?'

After a moment his father said, 'He won't move.'

Eric understood. Particularly with kelpies. They were faithful to one man, even unto death. So Eric began his usual loping run to the stockyard. He aleady knew where the buggy would be. It would be parked near the water tap where drovers usually camped out when they brought in sheep or cattle – which is where he found it: an old and battered buggy with five horses in the pen near it, and a frisky pony. Bob and Perce were boiling a billy on a kindling wood fire, and they seemed to be copies of his father: old men who moved slowly and spoke slowly and who hardly looked at him when he asked for his father's clothes bag. 'For Mr Thompson,' he said.

'Which one is it, Perce?' Bob said.

'That old army bag,' Perce said.

Bob rummaged in the buggy and gave Eric a sort of duffle bag which, though modest enough for a man, was not going to be easy for Eric to carry over a mile.

'And he wants some meat for the kelpie,' Eric remembered.

Perce simply dug his hand into a cut-away kerosene tin and came up with a mutton bone with a lot of cooked meat on it and, shooing the flies away, he handed it to Eric who was now trying to shoulder the clothes bag.

'Full of old boots,' Bob said laconically, smiling and revealing a mouth which was toothless. 'How far do you have to go?'

'About a mile and a bit,' Eric said.

'I'll give you a dink,' Bob said, and lifting a worn saddle

and blanket from the back of the buggy and throwing it complete on one of the horses in the stock pen, he bridled the horse, did up the girth buckles and mounted. He told Eric to give him the bag, which he put across the saddle in front of him, and then he said, 'Now put your left foot on mine and get up behind me.'

Eric lifted his foot but he couldn't reach the stirrup so Bob simply leaned over and pulled him up with a single tug. He swung Eric up behind and said, 'Don't hold my trousers. You'll pull them off. Put your arms around my waist if you have to, but don't do it unless you're going to fall off.'

And, like that, with Eric clutching the meat bone, Bob took him home silently and slowly in the early darkness as if this was no more than a moment's brief diversion in a lifetime of living on a horse. He dropped Eric at the gate of the house and though Eric said, 'Goodbye Bob,' Bob simply grinned his toothless grin and rode away. Eric took the clothes bag into the house, but when he was inside his mother said 'Shhh' and pointed to his father who was asleep fully-clothed on his mother's bed, his old face exhausted in sleep, his mouth open, his unseeing eyes closed now against the visible horizon he had spent a lifetime avoiding.

His mother closed the door and that should have been the moment to end Saturday, December 2, because Eric didn't see his father again. But the day didn't really end that way, because when he woke up on the Sunday Eric discovered that his mother was already awake and dressed, although it was only six o'clock, and that his father had gone.

'Yes, he's gone,' his mother said to him. 'But go out the back and see what your father left you.'

Eric ran outside to the sandy back yard which extended about twenty yards to a wooden fence, and at the end of the yard he saw a pony tied to his mother's clothes line. It was the same skittish pony he had seen at the stockyards. It whirled around nervously when Eric approached it. It was a dark chestnut colt, very dark, but not black. It had a star on its forehead, a bushy tail, and ears that twitched and nostrils that seemed to snort as he pulled back angrily on the rope halter that held him to the line.

Eric couldn't believe it.

He shouted, running back to the house where his mother was waiting at the door: 'Do you mean the pony? Is that what he left me?'

'Yes,' his mother said. 'And there's a bridle on the nail behind the door.'

'You mean he's mine? He left it for me?'

'Yes,' his mother sighed, watching her son closely. 'That's what he left for you. But your father says he's not yet broken in. He says you'll have to do it yourself. And you must go down first thing this morning to see Mr Richards. He will tell you what to do.'

Eric was still in a state of such disbelief that he hardly noticed that there were hidden tears in his mother's eyes as she walked back into the house.

Chapter 3

Mr Richards was a wholesale dealer in grain and feedstuffs and he had once been the best horseman in the town. But now he was arthritic and couldn't get on a horse, and these days he not only dealt in wholesale grain and feed but in meat and livestock and anything that came off the land. He was a very erect and serious man, a former soldier, an Anzac (a light-horse artilleryman) and a one-legged man. He had lost his right leg at Gallipoli in 1915 and now he had an artificial one with a creaking foot which seemed to have stiffened his manner as well as his leg. But he had a reputation for fierce honesty and no nonsense.

'Where's the pony?' he said sternly to Eric when Eric stood at his back door at nine o'clock that Sunday morning.

'I left him at home,' Eric said.

'Why? What's happened to him?'

'Nothing, Mr Richards. He's so wild that I was worried he'd break loose if I tried to lead him here. I can't ride yet.'

'That's not the way to start breaking him in. If you ever want to ride that pony you can't be afraid of him. Did your father tell you what the arrangement was?'

Eric shook his head vigorously. He had always been in awe of Mr Richards because he talked to Eric the way he talked to adults. He made no concessions for age.

'Your father should have told you,' Mr Richards said. 'All right. Get in the car and I'll take you home.'

Mr Richards' open Dodge tourer was only a few feet away and as Eric sat in the front seat Mr Richards called out to his

26

wife, 'I'll be back in half an hour, Mabel,' and got in the other side.

'D'you know my paddock down by the railway line, near the river?' he asked Eric as they turned into the main road.

'Where you keep old Dixie?' Eric said.

'That's right. You'll keep your pony there with my old grey. But first you'll have to get your pony down there, and after that I'll explain what you have to do.'

When they arrived at the house Eric called to his mother who came out wiping her hands from the soap suds of her weekly wash.

'Hello, Mr Richards,' she said.

'Good morning, Mrs Thompson,' he said. 'I'm just going to take the boy's pony down to my paddock near the railway line, and I'll explain to him what he has to do.'

'All right,' Mrs Thompson said. 'Would you like a cup of tea?'

'No thanks, Mrs Thompson,' Mr Richards said, and without any more talk he walked stiff and erect (though with a remarkable disguise of his limp) to the back of the yard while Eric had to run to keep up with him.

'Have you given the pony a name yet?' Mr Richards said.

'I haven't even thought about it,' Eric said. 'I haven't had time.'

'Call him Brownie,' Mr Richards ordered. 'He's brown enough. A real chestnut.'

They were now face to face with the pony who dilated his nostrils, twitched his ears, whirled around as if he would like to kick them, and then raised his head angrily and snorted.

'Don't take any notice of that,' Mr Richards said. 'He's putting it on, so don't let him frighten you. Be still,' he said to the pony who ignored him. 'Now listen,' he said to Eric. 'I'm not going to touch him. I'll tell you what to do and you do it. Understand?'

'Yes,' Eric said.

'Where's the bridle?'

'Inside.'

'Get it.'

'Am I going to ride him?' Eric said in a panic as the pony began to tug at the halter and plunge from one side to the other like a wild beast.

'No. Not yet. Get the bridle,' he said.

Eric ran to the verandah to get the bridle where his mother, worried and watching carefully, was holding it for him. He hardly saw her as he snatched the bridle and ran back with it.

'We'll leave the halter on him,' Mr Richards said, 'and we'll take him down to my paddock behind the Dodge, so you'll have to sit in the back to hold him.'

'I don't think I'm strong enough to hold him,' Eric pointed out.

'It's all in the mind,' Mr Richards said, tapping his forehead. 'Particularly with horses and dogs. You hold him, or he holds you. Which is it to be?'

'I'll hold him,' Eric said.

But when he untied the halter from the clothes line and pulled hard on it the pony balked and backed away.

'Hoss! Heroooch!' Mr Richards shouted, and the pony stopped pulling and reluctantly moved behind Eric. But as they passed the back verandah he shied and almost pulled Eric over.

'He's not going to ride that pony, is he Mr Richards?' Mrs Thompson said in a panic.

'He'll be all right, Mrs Thompson,' Mr Richards replied. 'Don't worry.'

But Mrs Thompson looked very worried as she followed them through the front gate and watched Eric get into the back of the open Dodge, still holding firmly to the halter rope. For a moment the pony seemed curiously docile, as if he liked this. But as Eric quickly tied the halter to the hood stays (the hood was down) and Mr Richards started the Dodge, the pony leapt back on its hind legs and tried to break free.

'Undo that halter,' Mr Richards shouted as he turned around and saw what Eric had done. 'Always hold a horse's lead in your hand. Never tie it to anything if you're moving.'

'I won't be able to hold him,' Eric shouted back.

'Try, for Pete's sake.'

Eric untied the rope and, facing backwards and wrapping the halter around his wrists, he hung on as the Dodge moved off.

Mr Richards' paddock was only a few minutes away, but to Eric it seemed like an hour as he held hard to the rebellious, unpredictable pony who was docile and soft for one moment then violent in resistance the next.

When they reached the paddock Mr Richards said: 'Good boy ...' to Eric. 'Now don't let him go. Hang on.'

In fact Eric's wrists were raw but he didn't care because he knew that somehow he had won a little victory over the pony, even though a moment later the pony leapt back, lifted his head, and pulled Eric over.

'Tcoooch. Hoss ...' Mr Richards shouted at the pony as he opened the wire gate and greeted his old black mare who had walked up sedately to greet her master.

'Now get him in,' Mr Richards told Eric who pulled, leaning back.

Eric repeated Mr Richards' cry: 'Tcooch. Hoss ...' and the pony with a gesture of toleration and condescension simply and surprisingly walked quietly into the paddock. But the moment he was inside he jerked his head violently so that Eric, caught unaware, lost the halter, and the pony galloped triumphantly around the paddock in a little victory ceremony of his own.

'Let him go,' Mr Richards said as Eric began to chase him. 'It's his paddock now, so let him feel he can do what he likes in it.'

'What about the halter, Mr Richards?'

'That won't hurt him for the time being. We'll get it off

him in a moment.' And as he closed the gate he said to Eric, 'We'll get him a bucket of feed in a minute, and then you can get at the halter. In the meantime come over here and I'll explain it all to you.'

Seated on the running board of the Dodge, Mr Richards told Eric that his father had picked up fifty head of sheep for him in Moorabin, New South Wales and cut them into the herd he was bringing to St Helen. Instead of payment for driving them here, Eric's father had asked Mr Richards to supply Eric with enough feed every day for the pony, and a place to keep him. Mr Richards had agreed on the condition that Eric kept the pony in the paddock with his old and beloved grey mare, Dixie, and that Eric should feed and water both horses twice a day, brush them down at least twice a week, and clean up the manure when it got a bit much.

'There's the shed with the chaff and oats in it,' Mr Richards said, pointing to a corrugated iron lean-to. 'I'll give you a key to the padlock and you just fill each of them a bucket with chaff and a half of oats and put it into the feed trough every morning and evening. And if they need it a little in the afternoon as well. And keep the water trough full, always full. Just turn the tap on, that's all you have to do. And if I ever hear that the water trough is empty I'll send you packing, d'you understand?'

'Yes, Mr Richards.'

'Any questions?' Mr Richards said in his military voice.

'Yes,' Eric said with genuine curiosity now that he was beginning to feel that he could speak to Mr Richards. 'Why do you call your old horse grey when Dixie is really black?'

'All black or white horses are called greys. Your pony is a chestnut, because he's brown. Now we'll give them a feed and I'll show you all that I intend to show you. The rest will be up to you.'

So Mr Richards showed Eric how to unlock the feed shed, scoop out the chaff and oats from the big bin, carry it (Eric staggered with it) to the trough and then, when the pony was busy eating, how to get the halter off.

'Let him finish, and then I'll show you how to bridle him.'

They waited for the pony to finish eating and, just before he began to lick the last flakes of chaff and oats from the smooth bottom of the tin trough, Mr Richards got a grip on his mane, and pulling the bridle up along the face and over the ears he pushed the bit into the pony's mouth with the flat of his hand and in a few seconds had the nose band and cheek strap done up.

'That's all there is to it,' he told Eric. He put two fingers between the pony's jaw and the cheek strap and said, 'Always allow a bit of space here, not too much because if it is too loose he'll get the bit in his teeth and you'll never stop him. If it's too tight you'll cut his mouth. You understand?'

'Yes,' Eric said. 'Not too loose and not too tight.'

'You haven't got a saddle, and you're not likely ever to have one,' Mr Richards went on, 'so you'll have to ride him bare back, which is the best way to learn anyway. But once you're up on him don't lean forward or backward. Keep yourself straight, and hold your reins where your hands fall naturally. If you have to hold on to something then get a grip on his mane. But never let go the reins, even if he throws you. Just hang on to them. And don't ride him on asphalt or hard ground. He isn't shod and he doesn't need to be.'

Eric looked at his pony, docile for a moment at the end of the bridle, and he said, 'How do I get on him?'

'That'll be your first problem. Get on him anyway you can, but always on his left side. Get him near the trough if you can and jump on him from that. But in time you'll learn to scramble on like a Red Indian.'

'He'll never stand still, Mr Richards. Look at him.'

When Mr Richards took the bridle off, the pony began to shy and prance again, and Mr Richards shrugged and said, 'You'll have to get the better of him yourself. You'd better

31

stick to the paddock until you're sure you can control him. And remember, it's your knees, your calves, your thighs and your heels that keep you on. Not your backside or your hands.'

And as Mr Richards gave him the key (on a chain) to the padlock, and left in his Dodge, Eric squatted on the ground and watched his pony for the rest of the morning (as indeed he had already watched him early morning before going to Mr Richards). In fact he knew that they were watching each other, he and his pony, as if they were both trying to decide if they were going to be perpetual enemies, or lifelong friends.

Chapter 4

Luckily it was summertime, and because there was no school Eric had plenty of time to spend with the pony. Every morning before breakfast he would run down to the paddock to make sure that the pony was still there, and when his mother guessed what was in his mind she said: 'Nobody's going to take him away, Eric. He's quite safe . . .' Eric said, 'I know that. But he's so clever and cunning that I'll bet he's trying to find a way of getting out.'

'Then make sure you close the gate tight,' Mrs Thompson said.

Eric nodded, and after breakfast he hurried through his chores – watering the violet bed and cutting enough box wood for the stove – before running back to the paddock.

Previously, whenever Eric had passed this paddock, he had always greeted Mr Richards' old grey mare Dixie over the wire fence, but now that he had the authority and the right to be inside the paddock he walked over to the old grey who was sheltering under a corrugated iron lean-to and said, 'Hello, Dixie. You don't eat much, do you?'

Eric stroked the chin and hard nose of the mare who stood perfectly still and accepted the affection without resistance or response. Now that he was close enough Eric could see in the old horse what had once been the sprightly black beauty that Mr Richards had ridden so superbly in the Anzac Day parades, which people still talked about.

But the real point of his affection for Dixie was his own provocation of the pony. Eric had already discovered the day before that the pony, like Eric himself, was very curious and that sooner or later he liked to take a look at whatever was going on. Sitting on the feed trough watching the pony sniff and snort around the paddock, Eric had been suddenly surprised by the pony approaching him and inspecting him closely as he sat there. Then suddenly dashing off again.

'Well, I'll be damned,' Eric had said.

Now, he petted the old mare deliberately to provoke the pony; not so much to arouse his curiosity but, 'If he sees me patting old Dixie, maybe he'll want some of it himself,' was Eric's thinking.

In fact when Dixie, who was lonely in her old age, followed Eric as he walked backwards, his hand still caressing her nose, the pony rushed up to join them irritably but determinedly.

'Come on,' Eric whispered to the mare.

The old mare followed slowly, and as the pony came closer and closer Eric went on saying loudly to the mare, 'Good old Dixie. Good old girl . . .'

Finally, when the pony came near enough for Eric to put out his hand to touch him, the pony allowed only the briefest of contacts before swerving away and galloping off wildly as if in protest.

'Well. It's a bit of a start,' Eric said, but he wondered how he would ever be able to put a bridle on the pony.

That night when Eric told his mother what he had been doing with the pony she listened very quietly and nodded and said 'Yes' or 'Good heavens' but she didn't ask him questions, and Eric was so excited about the pony that he didn't notice her reluctance or her secret looks at his happy face. Hers were not happy looks, they were worried and rather sad because there was no way she could tell her son that she was not only worried about his safety, but she did not want to watch him become a copy of his father – who, at Eric's age, was also put on a horse and left there.

34

'I saw Dora Hunt today,' she said to Eric and waited for his interest.

But Eric was thinking only of the pony; and without realizing it the rest of his interest in the town, including any news of Dora Hunt, was now forgotten.

The next morning he had a new idea about the pony. When the pony was busy feeding at the bin he took the brush from the feed shed and began to brush the pony's back. He managed two strokes before the pony moved irritably sideways. But Eric persisted, carefully brushing not only the back but the neck and saying, 'Whooa ...' and 'Tsteck' and inventing his own sounds of reassurance. The pony obviously liked it, but at the same time resented it and resisted it, and when he had finished his feed he lifted his head and ran off.

But he returned when Eric brushed down Dixie, who stood obediently and appreciatively still as Eric did a thorough job, using the curry comb to clean the brush the way he had seen Joe Hislop the blacksmith using it.

'You don't like being out of it, do you?' Eric said to the pony. 'But I'm not going to take any notice of you. I'm ignoring you.'

And he went on brushing Dixie until the pony couldn't stand it any longer. He rushed up and butted Eric with his nose before running away again.

Eric persisted with this method and on a quiet afternoon when it was very hot the pony's resentment and curiosity got the better of him and he came close enough for Eric to get a grip on his mane which the pony didn't resist, and Eric knew that he now had a chance to get a bridle on him.

He was walking quietly behind the pony with the bridle in his hand, making new noises, when he was hailed by a boy called Smiley MacLaughlin, an Irish boy a year older than Eric, who had arrived in the town two years ago but still spoke with a Kerry accent. His real name was Michael MacLaughlin but he had acquired his Australian nickname because no one had ever seen his small dark face break into a smile. And he never smiled because he seemed to have no reason to. He had no mother, and his cheerful, drunken father (a milk collector) beat him every day; and every day Smiley defied him. As a reaction to his beatings Smiley seemed determined to beat anybody else who challenged him: any boy who annoyed him or argued with him or questioned him or defied him, although it was a hopeless cause for Smiley because he was too small and thin and underfed to beat anybody. He had no chance against healthier, harder Australian boys, becuase the best he could do was to fight with his head down and his fists flying.

But it wasn't his fists or his head that worried his opponents, it was his big sloppy boots, which he wore without socks on this thin legs. The worst thing you could say to Smiley was that he was 'too big for his boots'. Say that to him and he would lash out with them. But it was literally true. He could hardly walk properly in them, and Mrs Halford, who knew so much about everybody in the town, would say to her son, Bob: 'I'm sure that boy Smiley sleeps in his boots . . .' To which Bob would reply: 'They smell . . .' To which Mrs Halford would add, 'Yes, because he is afraid someone will take them away from him so he never takes them off.'

'He fights like a starved cat,' Bob said.

In any case, though Smiley always lost his challenges and never fulfilled his threats of 'I'll get you later' it didn't deter him, though it did make everybody rather cautious with him, including his teachers.

'What are you doing?' Smiley shouted at Eric now.

'Trying to get a bridle on him,' Eric shouted back and regretted it immediately, because he knew what Smiley would do. Smiley had to bridle and harness his father's horse every morning at five o'clock, so he could claim to be an expert in horse-handling.

'You don't know how to do it,' Smiley said, and entering

the paddock he stamped over to Eric in his sloppy boots, snatched the bridle from him, and began to approach the pony in his usual threatening manner. Smiley was clearly telling the pony that if he didn't stand still it would be so much the worse for him.

'Whoa ... Stand still, you shifty beast,' Smiley shouted angrily.

The pony, who had been playing an amusing game with Eric by moving a little and stopping and moving again, had reached the point when he was willing to tolerate Eric's grip on his mane. But this new kind of approach was a rude intervention, and as Smiley came up on him from behind he turned around and plunged forward, knocking Smiley over as he galloped around the paddock.

'You foul beast,' Smiley shouted at him, getting up. 'I'll be after you for that.'

'You can't do it like that,' Eric told Smiley angrily. 'You'll only make him worse.'

'You don't know anything about it,' Smiley said.

'You don't know anything yourself,' Eric said. 'Leave him alone, Smiley.'

'Get out of my way,' Smiley ordered, pushing Eric aside.

He went after the pony on his small legs and big boots, swinging the bridle and shouting terrible threats. The pony was so alarmed that he carelessly backed himself into a corner, which allowed Smiley to get close to him.

'If you don't stand still I'll whip you,' Smiley was saying.

The pony retreated nervously, and when Smiley finally had him deep in the corner of the paddock the pony reared up on his hind legs, kicked out with his front legs, and then plunged foward again. This time he didn't knock Smiley over. Instead, he tried to bite Smiley's bare legs as he rushed by. Furious, Smiley aimed a late kick at him and began to swear and chase the pony again. This time he was swinging the bridle like a whip, and when he got near enough he lashed the pony across the face with it, not once but twice, and the pony seemed to scream in anger.

Eric was already after him, and somehow he got a grip on the bridle and told Smiley to let go. 'Don't hit him,' Eric shouted, tugging at the bridle. 'Just leave him alone.'

'He's not going to knock me over,' Smiley said. 'I'll get him.'

'No . . .'

Eric kept his grip on the bridle, and in the tug of war Smiley lashed out with his boots, catching Eric once on the bare shins. But Eric hung on, and though Smiley threatened to flatten him and went on aiming kicks at him, Eric had a good grip on the bridle and was shouting at Smiley, 'Let go. Give it up.'

Smiley now tried to stamp on Eric's bare feet, but Eric was too quick for him, and in their fierce little contest of footplay Smiley loosened his grip on the bridle and Eric snatched it free and ran off with it.

'Hand it over,' Smiley shouted, chasing him.

But the one defence that worked against Smiley was the nimble foot, because he couldn't run fast in his big boots. Eric easily eluded him.

'I'll get you, Snow,' Smiley kept shouting.

'Not me,' Eric said, keeping his distance.

'Tomorrow . . .' Smiley said, and turned his attention to the pony. He began to chase him, and though Eric thought of coming to the pony's aid, he realized that the pony was perfectly capable of looking after himself. When he wasn't avoiding Smiley he would suddenly swerve and kick out violently, missing Smiley by inches, and after ten minutes of this fruitless contest Smiley had to give up, exhausted. He tried to get at Eric who was also too quick for him, and finally when Smiley stamped off on his thin legs in their big boots, he shouted back at Eric: 'I'll get you yet, Snow. I'll get you when you're not looking.'

Eric said nothing, knowing it was a threat Smiley would soon forget, but when he went back to his attempt to get a grip on the pony's mane, he realized that Smiley had ruined everything he had achieved so far. The sight of the bridle after that lash across the nose was enough to send the pony off in an angry panic, so that Eric had to put the bridle down and try to soothe the pony with gentle words and quick strokes, which the pony now resisted.

'Don't blame me,' Eric said angrily to him. 'I didn't do it.'

But the damage was done and Eric knew he would have to think up some new way of dealing with this furious little horse.

That night, when he told his mother what had happened, she made what was to Eric an extraordinary suggestion. 'Maybe he's just too wild, Eric, so perhaps it would be better if you asked Mr Richards to sell him to somebody.'

Eric was so surprised that he didn't know what to say. 'You couldn't really sell him,' he said at last. 'You couldn't do that.'

'But he's too wild, Eric. You'll never be able to break him in.'

'Yes, I will,' Eric said. 'I'll think of something.'

'But even if you do ...' Mrs Thompson stopped there, because she still could not tell Eric her real thoughts and her real worries about him.

'I'll do it somehow,' Eric said. 'Don't worry.'

'I'm not really worried,' Mrs Thompson said with a sigh which seemed to contradict her words.

The next day it was still hot, and Eric sat on the feed trough watching the pony rolling in the dust. Eric knew, or guessed, that sooner or later he would want a drink and it gave him a new idea.

'Why don't I try to get on him without a bridle? He can't get out of the paddock, so the bridle won't help anyway. I can hang on to his mane.'

He moved to the water trough, and after the pony had

rolled around a few more times in the dusty corner he walked slowly to the water trough. Ignoring Eric, he began to suck the water noisily through his curled lips.

'Now . . .' Eric whispered to himself.

Moving cautiously he manoeuvered himself into a position just behind the pony's neck, and with a quick leap from the trough he flung himself onto the pony's back, falling forward on its neck. The pony stiffened, turned his head to see what had happened, and realizing that Eric was on his back he leapt forward on his front legs and began to race around the paddock as Eric held on with his legs and arms and hands and heels.

Eric felt the hard bone of the pony's back almost cutting him in two. He gripped the pony's mane and tried not to fall off as the pony swerved and twisted and then simply ran flat out towards the wire fence.

Eric was terrified for a moment that the pony was going to gallop straight into the fence. But on the very edge of it the pony stopped dead as if the world itself had stoppped so that Eric flew through the air, over the fence, and landed head over heels in the dust outside the paddock.

He was winded. He had scraped his knees and twisted an elbow, but as he sat up and rubbed his shins he noticed that the pony was watching him from the other side of the wire fence.

'You got me that time,' Eric said ruefully, 'but I'm going to do it again.'

As if to say, 'Oh no you're not,' the pony swung around and trotted calmly to the other end of the paddock.

Eric picked himself up and thought for a moment.

Limping back to the gate he decided on another tactic. He was sure that the pony was not only curious, but resentful of anything he did with old Dixie.

'You don't like to be left out of it, I already know that much,' Eric said aloud as he opened the door of the lean-to where the feed was stored.

On the dirt floor of the shed was a stout wooden box which had once been filled with .12 gauge Eley Shotgun cartridges but now contained some old horseshoes, a broken bridle and some buckles from a saddle girth. Eric tipped these out, and taking the box to where Dixie was standing half asleep, he stood on the box and scrambled up Dixie's front leg to her back.

'I hope Mr Richards won't mind, Dixie,' he said to the old horse. 'So just walk around a bit.'

He dug his heels lightly into Dixie's sides and Dixie obeyed as if she was glad to have someone on her back again without a saddle or a bridle. She walked slowly around the paddock, and when she came close to the pony she seemed deliberately to brush him. In any case the pony was now aware, and after Dixie's second circuit of the paddock the pony joined them with that rather irritable way he had of approaching something he resented.

'You see,' Eric told the pony, 'you're not the only pebble on the beach.'

The pony kept his distance but followed, and when Eric was least expecting it the pony came alongside and suddenly tried to bite his leg. Eric felt the wet lips, the rough teeth. He heard the snap of the teeth meeting. But he was too quick and he lifted his leg before the pony could have a second bite at him.

'Well, I'll be damned,' Eric said, which being his favourite expression of surprise or bewilderment or even appreciation was all he could say. But once he had recovered from his surprise he laughed because he knew that it was part of a mutual game they were now playing with each other. And he said again, 'Well, I'll be damned.'

Eric had to hurry home for his lunch, and after he had cleaned out the kitchen grate for his passionately clean mother who hated ashes, he was on his way out again when his mother said:

'Don't you go swimming any more, Eric? Or fishing?'

'Haven't time,' Eric said.

'But it's so hot.'

'I'll have a swim when I've finished. Goodbye . . .' he said.

'Goodbye,' his mother said and watched him disappear down the street, deciding at the same time that she would go down to the paddock herself to see what he was doing with the pony, although she knew it would only tell her the worst, no matter what he was doing.

By now Eric knew that his only hope was to stick close to the pony so that when the opportunity arose he could leap on his back and simply stay on somehow. So he took the little Eley box with him and followed the pony around the paddock, knowing that the pony was playing a game with him and was teasing him rather than resisting him.

Twice Eric managed to put the box down and then take a flying leap at the pony's back. But the pony leapt clear and Eric fell in the dirt. On the third attempt he devised a method of running with the box, putting it down, stepping quickly on it and leaping onto the pony – all in one manoeuvre. It worked, and he hung on with his legs and feet and heels as the pony galloped around the paddock. But every time the pony came close to the wire fence and was about to stop on a sixpence and throw him over it, Eric kicked him hard with one foot or the other and the pony swerved away. The pony threw him again, but Eric persisted and, as if there had to be a compromise in any game, the pony seemed less and less anxious to get rid of him. Rather he seemed determined to scare him with swerves and little jumps and noisy snorts.

Eric came off again and again, but by the end of the afternoon he was able to take a quick run and jump on the pony's back without the box; and when he could do that Eric knew that he was half-way to success.

The real problem was still the bridle.

Each time the pony saw the bridle he made it clear that he

was afraid of it, and hated it, and it was Mrs Thompson who gave Eric the simple idea that solved the problem. She came down to the paddock in the afternoon to see what Eric was doing and when she saw him stalking the half-wild pony and hurling himself at its neck and somehow getting on board as it exploded from its four feet, she didn't know whether to laugh or cry because it looked both funny and dangerous. When he was thrown she didn't cry out, although she wanted to. She simply held her hand to her mouth and rushed across the paddock to see if he was hurt.

'It's all right,' Eric said as he got up. 'I'm not hurt.'

Mrs Thompson closed her eyes for a moment and hoped that her eleven-year-old son was supple and light and relaxed enough to take the sort of physical punishment that an older person couldn't.

'You shouldn't do it without a bridle, Eric,' she told him. 'You can't control the pony without one. You *have* to get the bridle on him.'

Eric had already told his mother about the difficulties with the bridle, and now that she had seen the risks he was taking she gave him the solution to the pony's resistance.

'Just hang the bridle over the feed bin,' she told him, 'then he'll get used to it and stop being afraid of it.'

Eric thought it a marvellous idea and he looped the bridle over the feed bin for the next few days, so that the pony eventually took no notice of it. After a few clumsy attempts which failed, Eric finally got the bridle on him while he was feeding, and when the pony had finished eating Eric leapt on his back and at last had reins in his hands, even though the chin strap was loose and even though he dare not pull hard on the reins in case he pulled the bridle right off.

It didn't take Eric long to get the bridle on thereafter, but he could only do it when the pony was feeding, which he didn't like. It was his mother who again told him a simple way.

'Horses always like bread,' she told Eric, 'so give him a little piece of bread when you put the bridle in his mouth. Then you can always persuade him to take the bridle.'

Again Eric tried it, and again it worked.

So the day finally came when Eric could bridle the pony and leap on his back and race around the paddock without coming off more than once or twice. And though Eric felt as if he had won something (me instead of you) he knew that the pony was making his own sport of it. Which was how they began to know each other.

But that was only the beginning of the change in Eric's life, not the end.

Chapter 5

The town now began to see Eric on the pony, and from the outset it was a transformation from a quicksilver boy into a quicksilver pony – with a boy on him. They didn't see much of him at the beginning because he kept away from the town, so they didn't see the continuing day-by-day contest as the pony tried to outwit Eric and Eric tried to out-think the pony. Instead, they saw a flash from time to time as Eric and the pony appeared and disappeared. But eventually, even before the middle of summer, it was hard to think of one without the other because it was now rare to see Eric without the pony.

'You know, Bob,' Mrs Halford said to her son when she saw Eric appear and disappear one day, 'that pony has saved the Thompson boy.'

'What do you mean?' the sceptical Bob said.

'He's finally got a real friend of his own,' Mrs Halford said.

'Funny sort of friend,' Bob said. 'Horses can't even talk.'

'No. But if you watch that boy and his pony you can see that they understand each other perfectly. It's very nice to just look at them tearing down the street.'

'But he keeps being thrown off,' Bob pointed out.

'That's because the pony is a cocky little thing. It's just what Eric needed. It's finally given him some confidence.'

'Being chucked off?' Bob demanded.

'No. Getting back on again,' his mother replied.

In fact it was soon obvious to every one in town that not only were the boy and the pony inseparable, but that Eric himself had changed somewhat. Even though he was seen more and more in the town, he came and went so mysteriously and so quickly that nobody seemed to know where he was going or what he was doing.

When for instance Mrs Halford called out to him from her front garden as he was riding by at a quick trot, 'Hello, Eric,' and then walked over to the fence to try to talk to him, Eric simply rode on and shouted jerkily, 'Hello, Mrs Halford.'

'Doesn't that pony ever walk?' Mrs Halford called after him because she wanted to ask him about the pony, and where on earth he was always going with it.

'Can't stop now,' Eric called over his shoulder as he rode on. 'Goodbye, Mrs Halford.'

'Goodbye, Eric.'

It was like that with other people he normally stopped to talk to. Now these old familiars, and others too, seemed to take some pleasure in greeting Eric, even though he would simply wave a friendly hand and call out a reply in passing. The more this sort of thing happened the more an interested observer, like Mrs Halford, wondered about it until she finally gave Bob her own explanation of it.

'I think he's afraid that if he stops too long somebody will take the pony away from him.'

'What would they do that for?' Bob said. 'It's his pony.'

'When you're poor,' Mrs Halford said, 'and when you've suddenly been given something very precious, sooner or later you expect it to be taken away from you.'

'That's silly,' Bob said.

'Nonetheless I'll bet that's what he really feels, even though he isn't aware of it himself.'

The two people whom Eric would stop and talk to were Father O'Connel and Dora Hunt. Every time Father O'Connel saw him on the pony he would shout, 'Whoaaa up there. Get off your horse, young Thompson.'

It was a Friday, and this time Eric came to a sudden dusty full stop and was off the pony's back in a split second.

'What's the hurry? Where are you off to?' Father O'Connel said.

'Nowhere, Father.'

'Nonsense.'

'Well I was just going down to the stockyards.'

'What the devil do you want down there?' Father O'Connel said.

'There are three new horses in there for the Riverain Station.'

'You don't say,' Father O'Connel said with mock amazement. 'And what are you going to do with them? Break them in?'

Eric laughed. 'Not me, Father. Mr Richards told me to go and take a look at a good stock horse to see what it was like.'

'You don't say,' Father O'Connel said again. 'So it's all horses now, is it? Like your old man.'

'What do you mean, Father?'

'What's happened to all your old friends? Why are you neglecting them?'

Like Mrs Halford, Father O'Connel knew a great deal about what was going on in the town. It was Pat Radford of the butter factory who had remarked to him that the barefooted Thompson boy had stopped dropping in on her from time to time.

'I think I miss him,' she had said. 'Is he all right?' She had not heard then about the pony.

Now Father O'Connel said to Eric, 'Why don't you drop in on Pat Radford at the butter factory any more?'

'I haven't got time,' Eric said.

'Don't tell me that,' the Father said. 'What's the real reason?'

Eric was embarrassed, but he felt that he had to tell the truth. 'What would I do with the pony at the butter factory?'

'Tie him up outside,' Father O'Connel said.

'Mr Lewis wouldn't like that. He'd get them to take the pony off to the pound.'

'You can always get away quick. Go and say hello to Pat. She gets lonely in that place all day, just slapping up butter like mud pies.'

'All right, Father.'

While Eric had been talking to Father O'Connel the pony had been moving restlessly to and fro. He had finally turned his rump to Father O'Connel and, knowing the pony's tendency to be jealous of everybody, Eric had quickly pulled him around before he could let out a kick, saying secretly to himself and the pony: 'You're not going to get away with that.'

Before the pony could think up some new way of threatening Father O'Connel, Eric leapt on his back and at the same moment the pony swerved and was instantly into a full canter down the street.

'I think I'll call on that boy's mother,' Father O'Connel decided as Eric disappeared in a perfect cloud of St Helen's street dust.

It was different with Dora Hunt because Dora was so impressed with the pony that she wanted to know his name, and how old he was. And because she knew something about horses from her father and mother – how many hands he was (which Eric didn't know).

'But what do you call him?' she said.

'Mr Richards says I should call him Brownie,' Eric told her. 'But I don't call him anything at all.'

In fact Eric had discovered that he didn't want to give the pony a name because he knew that the connection between him and the pony was better than a name. There was no way he could call the pony Brownie any more than the pony could call him Eric. A name was superfluous because their contact was too complicated and close for one of them to impose a name on the other.

'Why don't you call him Brownie?' Dora persisted.

'I don't know. Maybe he wouldn't like it.'

'That sounds silly.'

'Well he's him, and I'm me . . .'

'Do you always ride him bareback?' she asked.

'Of course.'

'But wouldn't you like to ride him with a saddle?'

Eric shook his head. 'I'd hate a saddle. He'd hate it too.'

'My father says it's a pity you haven't got a saddle.'

'Well, I haven't got one,' Eric said, and with his usual flinging leap, which meant that he had only one leg barely hooked over the back of the pony as it moved off, Eric disappeared like a Red Indian down the street and out of sight.

From time to time Eric had wished that he did have a saddle, but the more he rode the pony, and the closer they came together in their mysterious contact with each other, the more Eric realized that his real link with the pony depended on that bare back. Eric's backside, heels, calves and even his knees were an essential link with the pony, telling him what to do, so that if Eric shifted his weight a little back or forward or sideways, the pony knew what it meant: a touch with the heel, a squeeze of the knees, a queer whistle, a sway, the slightest move . . . When Eric was sitting on that bare back they became one and the same animal. In the end even the reins seemed less important than this unthinking physical connection because Eric no longer thought of what he was doing. It was automatic and unconscious.

For his part the pony accepted the boy on his back and obeyed the instructions which the small agile body gave him. But he also kept his independence by refusing to be predictable. He seemed to take pride in sudden surprises, and as often as he could he would try his tricks on Eric.

Eric tried to explain it to Mr Richards who asked him if the pony still had his vicious little habits. 'Is he still playing up?'

'Yes, but he's not vicious, Mr Richards,' Eric said. 'He's just stubborn. He likes to do what he wants to do, that's all.'

'Explain that,' Mr Richards ordered.

'Well ... he's always pretending,' Eric said. 'He pretends to be frightened of a piece of paper or a dog or a car, so he tries to shy or bolt. Sometimes he tries to turn left when I want him to go right. But you can usually tell when he's going to do something bad because he flattens his ears down. Only he doesn't always do that when he suddenly swings around and tries to bite my leg. I never know when he's going to do that, so I have to be pretty quick.' And Eric went on to mention his other habits: trying to get the bit between his teeth, swerving into the paddock whenever he came near it, stopping dead when he felt like it, and simply taking off before Eric was even half mounted. 'He never lets me get up properly.'

'Does he still throw you off?' Mr Richards asked.

'Sometimes he does, but I can always tell when he wants to get me off. He moves sideways a little, so I dig my heels in.'

'Well, he's in good shape. So is Dixie. So keep it up, and don't let anyone else ride him. A good horse is a one-man animal. He's no use with two masters.'

Eric said he had no intention of letting anyone else near him. Ever!

'And keep him out of town. It's no place for an unshod pony.'

'Yes, Mr Richards.'

In fact Eric's only connection with the town now, apart from his Saturday jobs, was to pass through it. Before, when he had no pony, he seldom went into the real open countryside. He knew the river and the country that went beyond his end of the town. But apart from that he had always been a town boy. On the pony's back, however, he had become a country boy, and most of his rides now were journeys of exploration into empty spaces: the long and dusty Mallee roads, the open farmlands, the far-away corners of the little river and wherever else he could follow the dirt roads and tracks that led somewhere into the open, though he did not always know where. He became a familiar sight to the isolated farmers, the market gardeners, the irrigation people, the road men.

But the place he and the pony loved best was the wild end of Pental Island, where the country disappeared into itself. They usually aimed for Kelly's clump because Ned Kelly, the bush ranger, was supposed to have camped there, and beyond the big clump of gums the boy and the pony lost themselves in snake-infested country which was dangerously thick with lumps of spinifex grass, deep holes, rabbit warrens and the pitfalls and hazards that tested their mutual courage and their perfect co-ordination. The pony rarely stumbled, and in this country never deliberately tried to throw Eric. In fact they both accepted the difficult country as a challenge, and in their enjoyment of it they were fearless.

Even snakes didn't bother them. The first time the pony saw a snake, a six-foot black snake coiled up neatly on the dirt track, he knew instinctively what it was and simply swerved around it without any help from Eric who hadn't seen it. Thereafter when they saw a snake, sometimes coiled or sometimes slithering away, the pony would pull the reins forward and take his own head to avoid it. The only thing that did unnerve them was their one encounter with a five-foot goanna. Goannas were fearless, fast and aggressive, and they met this one under a patch of gum trees. Every boy in St Helen knew that by reputation a goanna, when confronted with a horse, would simply run up its front legs. When Eric saw the thick grey reptile confronting them threateningly he panicked and pulled hard on the reins. The pony also panicked and simply stood up high on his hind legs so that Eric came off. The pony tried to bolt, but Eric held the reins, and though he was dragged for a while, the pony soon recovered his nerve and stopped. Then Eric was on him in a flash and they were away as fast as the pony's legs could carry them.

But there was always a residual problem to these pleasures

of the bush. Sometimes Eric came home late, and he would find his mother waiting at the front gate for him. He knew it was wrong, and when his mother said to him, 'When you go off into the bush like that and come home late, I keep thinking you've been thrown somewhere and can't get up.'

He said, 'Yes, Mum,' and promised himself that he wouldn't come home late again. He did so once or twice, but in general he kept to his own promise. He knew, too, that his mother really wanted him to stick to the town, but Eric had abandoned the town – except for his Saturday jobs.

When he went early on Saturday mornings to Mrs Sansom's orchard he tied the pony to a post behind the tennis courts of the Presbyterian Church which was opposite. At the butcher's, Mr MacAllister told Eric to put the pony in the old stable behind the shop, where a long time ago the previous owner had kept a horse and buggy for delivery. And behind Mr Hunt's grocery store there was a large yard where Eric could tie the pony to a long high line that gave the pony enough movement to satisfy his restlessness. It was really Mr Hunt himself who had suggested the line.

From time to time when they passed each other on the road Mr Hunt had called out his usual greeting to Eric and sometimes had called after him, 'Wait a minute young Snow. I want to talk to you.'

But Eric had always sped on with a wave of his hand.

Behind his own shop, however, Mr Hunt had plenty of time to inspect the pony and to compliment Eric on his beautiful condition because Eric brushed him every day so that his coat shone. For some reason (though he didn't know why) Eric was afraid of Mr Hunt's admiration. He knew that Mr Hunt was an honest man, and according to his mother he was a good man. But somehow Eric was afraid, and he tried to avoid Mr Hunt when he came to the store to weigh up Slash's potatoes.

One Saturday in mid-summer when Dora came to the store, she told Eric that she wanted to see the pony. 'He's out there,' Eric said. 'You can see him if you want to.'

'No. I want you to come out. He just moves away when I try to get near him.'

'All right,' Eric said.

He left the potatoes and went outside with Dora. As he approached the pony he made some of the complicated little noises he now used in his talk to the pony. He changed the sounds almost every day. But the pony pricked his ears and came towards him.

'Oh he's lovely,' Dora said as Eric held the bridle and pushed and pulled and rubbed the restless pony until he stood still enough for Dora to rub his nose and chin. 'I wish I could ride him,' Dora said.

'He'd throw you off,' Eric told her.

'My father says it's time I had a pony of my own. He's going to get me one when I go back to school.'

'Where from?' Eric asked.

'I don't know. He's looking for a specially good one, so he might go over to the Riverain and ask them to sell him one of theirs.'

Eric had no intention of getting involved in Dora's hopes for a pony. For some inexplicable reason he didn't even want to know about it, so when Mr Hunt came through the yard and saw them with the pony Eric tried to hurry inside to finish weighing Slash's potatoes.

'Hold on,' Mr Hunt told him. 'What's the hurry?'

'I'm busy, Mr Hunt,' Eric said. 'I have to go now.'

'Never mind that,' Mr Hunt said with a smile. 'I want to put Dora up on your pony.'

'No. No,' Eric said in a panic. 'He'll throw her off, Mr Hunt. Don't do it.'

'I'll hold her,' Mr Hunt said. 'Don't worry.'

53

'But she wouldn't know what he was going to do,' Eric said.

'I know he's a bit skittish,' Mr Hunt said. 'But she'll be all right.'

'No, she won't. He'll throw her off.'

'How do you know he will?' Mr Hunt persisted.

'I just know. Don't get on him, Dora,' Eric said in a direct appeal.

'All right, if you don't want me to,' Dora said.

'What if I bring you a saddle? Can we put her up on him then?' Mr Hunt said, amused at Eric's resistance.

'I don't know, Mr Hunt. He's never had a saddle on him.'

'Well, let's try him one day,' Mr Hunt said. 'He's a beautiful little pony, Snow, and I like the way you ride him.'

Eric rubbed one bare foot on the other and longed to get back to his potatoes. But then Mr Hunt said something that Eric seemed to have expected and dreaded.

'Would you like to have him, Dora?' he said to his daughter.

'Oh yes,' Dora said. 'But he's Eric's.'

'How about selling him, Snow?' Mr Hunt said cheerfully.

Eric's left foot stopped rubbing his right foot, and he didn't know what had happened to him. But whatever it was it had paralysed him, as if some premonition had finally come true. He was so stunned that he could not say anything.

'I'll talk to your mother if you like,' Mr Hunt said.

Eric wanted to leap on the pony and disappear and never come near Mr Hunt's grocery store ever again. But knowing that if he did that he would lose his two shillings from Slash, he turned and ran inside the store, and when Dora eventually joined him he wouldn't look up from the potatoes when she said: 'You wouldn't really sell him, would you?'

Eric shook his head.

'That's what I told my father,' Dora said. 'He's your pony.'

Eric nodded, head down.

'I won't ever let him buy little Brownie,' she said. 'Honest.'

Eric buried his head in the potatoes. Realizing that he

wouldn't talk, Dora left him to his misery, which Eric suffered but did not understand. After all, the pony was still his. And Dora had promised not to allow her father to even think of buying him. And, if it came to that, he didn't have to sell the pony.

Nevertheless he knew that he and the pony were somehow at risk, though he didn't know what the risk was. And, as it turned out, the final effect of Mr Hunt's interest in the pony was not the one Eric was now afraid of. If anything the eventual result was quite unexpected, and, in its own way, much worse than his fear of Mr Hunt and his money.

Chapter 6

The trouble began when Mr Hunt told Eric one Saturday morning to leave the potatoes and come outside to the back of the store. Pointing to a pony saddle which was standing on its nose on an old fruit box, Mr Hunt said to Eric:

'There you are, Snow. I thought you'd like to have a go with a saddle. You can borrow it for a couple of weeks if you like, providing you look after it and lock it up every night in the feed shed.'

Even at first glance Eric liked the look of the little saddle, even though it was an old one, and seeing it like that, so near, he wanted suddenly to try it out. But once again something warned him not to touch it.

'I don't know how to ride with a saddle,' he told Mr Hunt.

'I know that. But I'll show you all you need to know. And the way you ride that pony you'll take to it like a duck to water.'

'Yes, but what if the pony doesn't like it?' Eric said unhappily.

'It won't take him long to get used to it.'

Eric thought for a moment and tried another way out. 'My mother wouldn't let me borrow a saddle like that, Mr Hunt. It might get lost or something.'

'I've spoken to your mother. She says you're pretty careful with your things. So when you've finished with Slash's potatoes I'll put you up on the saddle and show you the rudiments.'

'Well ... I don't know ...' Eric said, wriggling with discomfort and doubt.

'Give it a try, son. And if you're as good as I think you are I've got a suggestion to make. There's always a pretty good reason for my generosity,' he said in his cheerful way.

'You want the pony for Dora,' Eric blurted out.

Mr Hunt laughed outright. 'It's nothing to do with Dora,' he said. 'You just try it out and I'll tell you later what I've got in mind. I'm pretty sure you'll like the idea because you're wasting yourself and the pony just riding around like a Red Indian. I've got something better in mind, and it'll be good for the pony too.'

'You're not going to ask my mother to sell him, are you?' Eric said still in something of a panic.

Again Mr Hunt laughed. 'Nothing like that,' he said. 'You try the saddle and I'll tell you afterwards what's in my mind.'

And because he was so relieved that Mr Hunt was not trying to buy the pony, Eric agreed to try the saddle.

'But no taking it to school,' Mr Hunt said.

Eric shook his head.

The dry and parched summer of the Mallee was over and Eric was already back at school, and so far, instead of rushing down to the paddock every morning to leap on the pony's back and disappear, he was simply visiting the pony and Dixie early morning to feed and water them. Then he left them, which puzzled the pony. Why was Eric leaving him like this – imprisoned all day in the paddock? He nudged and pushed Eric when he was filling the bins; and when Eric closed the wire gate the pony put his head over the top and snorted and made a fuss with his feet and legs.

'I've got to go to school,' Eric explained every day. 'I'll be back at half past four.'

In fact he had discussed with his mother the idea of riding the pony to school, but his mother was against it.

'You'll just ride him there and ride him back, and the rest of the time he will be closed up in that little corner of the school yard.'

There were several older country boys who came to school in buggies and gigs, and they kept their horses in a corner of the school yard especially set aside for them. But they were there all day, and the boys brought feed bags in their buggies and gigs. Whereas Eric knew that he couldn't feed the pony in the school yard, and anyway he agreed with his mother. It was a confinement the pony would hate, because the school yard was much smaller than the paddock.

Nonetheless he couldn't resist the idea, and one Monday morning he had arrived at school with the pony and turned it loose in the corner enclosure, hanging up the bridle with the rest of the tack from the buggies and gigs. But he had not counted on the other boys, the town boys, who had never been able to get near the pony when he was on it, and were too afraid of Mr Richards to venture into the same paddock where Dixie was kept. At school thereafter, the pony was suddenly exposed to inspection, and eventually to teasing. The town boys discovered that by throwing up their arms in his face the pony would rise up on his back legs and paw the air in anger or fear, snort fiercely, and try to run around the confined space.

And there was also little Smiley in his big boots who had been waiting to pay Eric back, even though it was never his intention to do so. The pony fascinated him, and Smiley was the chief provocateur until the inevitable happened. At four o'clock one afternoon he reached the enclosure before Eric. He managed to bridle and mount the pony, and after opening the gate he was off at full gallop as Eric arrived at the enclosure.

'You're mad,' he shouted after Smiley. 'He'll only throw you off.'

'To blazes with you,' Smiley shouted over his shoulder.

But Eric called to the pony with one of his secret and curious noises. In an instant the pony did a complete turn on his hind legs, throwing Smiley, who rolled over and over in the dirt road as the pony trotted back neatly to Eric. And because he and Eric were in such instinctive co-operation he was obviously very pleased with what he had done. In fact the other boys who had seen it were laughing at Smiley and admiring the pony's skill and independence.

But Eric was on his back and away at a gallop almost before Smiley had picked himself up. 'I told you to leave him alone,' Eric shouted as he went by Smiley.

'I'll get you for this,' Smiley called after him.

'Not me,' Eric said as he disappeared.

Thereafter he left the pony in the paddock with Dixie during the day and let him out at half past four, after school, when he put the bridle on the pony, opened the gate, and like mad things released from prison they were off down the dirt road. On wings. Through the dust.

So it was superfluous now of Mr Hunt to warn Eric not to take the saddle to school. When Eric had finished weighing the potatoes he stood by silently, waiting for Mr Hunt who was packing tins on the shelves. Then they went out to the back of the store, and while Eric held the pony, Mr Hunt threw the saddle on him.

'He'll chuck it off,' Eric said.

The pony did so.

'Hit him lightly on the nose if he does that again,' Mr Hunt said.

'That'll only make him worse,' Eric replied.

'Well hold him still.'

'He never stays still.'

'In that case lift his head up with the bridle next time he tries to throw the saddle off.'

Eric did so and in that moment of hesitation Mr Hunt had thrown the saddle on the pony's back and grasped the girth strap and pulled it under the belly to the buckles. As the pony moved irritably away Mr Hunt tightened the girth and the saddle was on.

'He's a little devil, isn't he?' Mr Hunt said, panting with the effort.

'He's got a mind of his own,' Eric said, which was a repetition of something his mother had said of the pony.

'There's nothing wrong with that,' Mr Hunt said, 'so long as he doesn't make a fool of you. Now, put your left foot in the stirrup and pull yourself up by the saddle.'

Eric put his bare foot in the stirrup and in a moment he was up on the saddle as the pony tried his usual bursting take off. But this time Mr Hunt had such a firm grip on his head and bridle that he couldn't do it. And as he held the restless, indignant pony he said to Eric, 'You ought to wear shoes if you're riding with a saddle. Haven't you got a pair?'

'Yes, but ...' Eric was going to say that he had a pair of shoes but they were too good to be used for riding. 'I'll be all right.'

'Well watch your toes,' Mr Hunt said, and he then told Eric what he should do with the saddle. Press forward with the knees, inwards and forward, but backwards and inwards with the legs when he wanted to stop. He told Eric how to hold his hands and feet, how to calculate which leg the pony should start off on, etc. But then he suddenly changed his mind. 'Forget everything I've just said, Snow, and you go on riding him the way you've been riding him. Only remember you've lost your leg contact and your backside contact. He can't feel you, so you'll have to find your own way to hold him and control him with the bridle. It's different, very different, but your bareback riding should make it a piece of cake.'

In fact Eric was uncomfortable on the saddle. It was like sitting astride a restless chair: it had nothing living in it. And though he could feel a little of the pony with his bare heels, he was, as Mr Hunt said, suddenly aware of the reins and the bit. The rest of the living contact was lost, and the pony felt it too because he suddenly swung his head around, despite Mr Hunt's grip on the bridle, and before Eric could lift his leg the pony had nipped him.

'You little devil,' Mr Hunt said, laughing and pulling back the pony's head.

'He doesn't like it,' Eric said as the pony strained at the bridle.

'Off you go then,' Mr Hunt said, and as Eric turned the pony with his heels, and as they exploded through the gate and down the lane, Mr Hunt shook his head and said, 'A couple of Red Indians.'

In fact Eric no longer felt like a Red Indian, and the pony too seemed more determined than ever to contradict him. The pony suddenly insisted on trotting, which was not a gait either of them liked for very long.

'Don't trot,' Eric shouted at him and tried some of the various noises which normally produced a light ambling canter in a second. But without his knees and the pressure of his thighs and backside and subtle weight shifting, the pony ignored him, and Eric bounced up and down on the hard saddle.

'Where did you get the saddle?' Jack Scott the mechanic shouted as he passed in his Willys.

'Mr Hunt loaned it to me,' Eric said, bobbing up and down.

'You look like a fly on a beer barrel,' Jack laughed.

Eric had not yet learned to rise to the trot, and as he began to do so the pony deliberately varied his gait as if to defeat him.

'No, you don't,' Eric said and dug his heels in so that instinctively the pony cantered, then galloped, and Eric knew that a new contest of wills had begun. In fact the more the pony disobeyed him and tried to trick him, the more determined Eric was to make him accept the saddle and respond to it.

'It's you or me,' Eric said grimly to the pony.

At the paddock the pony tried to swing towards the fence because it was lunch time and that was what he normally did. But Eric pulled hard on the rein and stopped him, which made the pony so resentful of the change in their working programme that he tried to throw Eric. But the one advantage to the saddle and the stirrups was that Eric's feet were attached, so the old tricks wouldn't work and he stayed on.

'You see,' Eric said angrily. 'You can't throw me off with this saddle. Not that way.'

And as Eric began to use the reins rather than his body, the gap between him and the pony seemed to widen because the pony would grudgingly obey the reins but almost immediately disobey again by shying at nothing and putting his head down as if he were trying to pull the reins out of Eric's hands. Sometimes he deliberately crossed his front legs on a turn, so that he stumbled.

'You're doing that on purpose,' Eric said angrily as he forcefully lifted the pony's head. 'You'll only break your leg if you do that.'

The pony understood the words because, like a dog, he responded to the tone and the voice itself. When Eric finally took the saddle off and made an affectionate and conciliatory noise to the pony, the pony ran off without his usual affectionate nudge, and as if to wipe the feel of the saddle off his back he rolled over and over in the dust, which Eric knew was a vigorous protest against it.

'You're just being stubborn,' Eric said as he put the saddle away and locked the tin shed and went home. 'Stubborn, that's what you are,' he said to himself.

That night, when Eric and his mother exchanged their usual news, Eric told her about the saddle and the pony's behaviour, and she said, 'But you're much safer with a saddle.'

'It's different,' Eric said.

'You won't fall off so much,' Mrs Thompson insisted.

'I don't fall off, Mum. He throws me off.'

'Well he won't throw you off so often.'

'I know,' Eric said. 'But it's like starting all over again. It's funny.'

In the next few weeks Eric did begin all over again. He had to change his method of riding, and change the pony's responses to it. But slowly he succeeded in disciplining the pony to the impersonal lump of the saddle and to the loss of the old physical contact between his lightweight, flexible, responsive body and the restless, sensitive and stubborn horseflesh under him. But it had to be done on the comparative safety of dirt roads and smooth tracks without pitfalls.

It was Mr Hunt who was most satisfied. 'You've done a marvellous job, old son. He's saddle broke and you ride him like a veteran.'

It was Saturday and they were standing in the back yard of Mr Hunt's store. Dora was with her father, smiling happily as if she knew that her father was now about to reveal his original plan for Eric and the pony.

'What I'd like to do, Snow,' Mr Hunt said, 'is enter you in the Agricultural Show next month for the best pony and rider event. You'll have plenty of competition from the country boys and maybe from the Riverain crowd. But you ought to win hands down if you keep getting the better of your excitable little friend, Brownie. And there's a five-pound prize, which your mother could do with.'

Eric remembered last year's Agricultural Show, which he had visited through a hole in the high wooden fence (like most of the other bare-foot boys of the town). The Agricultural Show was held every year in the showgrounds and lasted two days. It was a big event for the whole area, because the town of St Helen was really a market town and railhead for the mixture of farming spreads all around it. There were not only displays of wheat, sheep, young cattle and beef, but citrus and dried fruits from the vineyards, sideshows, dairy and domestic (home-made) products, as well as buck jumping (Rodeo), horsemanship, show jumping, and pony events. And what Eric remembered of the pony events were the neat jodhpurs and polished boots and new white shirts of most (though not all) of the children competing.

'I wouldn't be able to ride in the showgrounds, Mr Hunt,' Eric said. 'I haven't got any of those jodhpurs and those proper boots.'

'You don't need jodhpurs and boots,' Mr Hunt told him. 'Just a white shirt and a pair of blue shorts and some shoes and socks.'

'I don't know if my mother will let me wear my best clothes riding,' Eric said.

'Don't worry. I'll talk to her about that,' Mr Hunt said.

'No, I'll do that,' Eric said quickly. 'But I wouldn't know what to do in there. They ride around poles.'

'I've got a little course set up over at Bob Miller's place. All you have to do is ride in and out of the pylons and take a couple of low jumps and start and stop when the judge tells you to. It's all a matter of timing, and that's what you've got plenty of.'

'How much will it all cost?' Eric asked.

'Nothing at all. I'll fix that. But you'll have to get your pony shod. I've fixed it up with Joe Hislop, the blacksmith. So you can go along there any time and he'll put shoes on the pony for you.'

'I don't know . . .' Eric said doubtfully.

'Oh go on,' Dora told him. 'I know you'll win. Everybody says you're the best pony rider ever.'

Eric was flattered and embarrassed and doubtful and worried. 'You can't tell what the pony will do if he has a lot of people around him all the time. He'll probably bolt or smash something.'

'That's up to you,' Mr Hunt said. 'But I think you'll manage him all right.'

'Of course you will,' Dora said enthusiastically. 'He'll do exactly what you tell him to.'

Eric wanted to say that with the saddle on him the pony's responses were strange and different and no longer trustworthy, but he didn't want to betray the pony by saying a thing like that, so he rubbed one foot on the other and tried to think of a new argument. There was only one possibility left.

'I'll ask my mother,' he said.

'I've already asked her,' Mr Hunt said. 'I happened to be down your way this morning and she said you can do it if you want to. So how about it?'

'Oh, go on,' Dora said again.

Eric knew there was no more retreat for him, so he said, 'All right. I'll have a go.'

'Good on you, Snow,' Mr Hunt said and gave Eric an affectionate slap on the back. 'You'll have that five pounds in your pocket before you or I can say Jack Robinson.'

In fact, as welcome as five pounds would be to his mother, Eric had not so far thought about the money. He had never considered the pony in connection with money, except the fear of Mr Hunt wanting to buy him. If anything, the pony was the very opposite to money, and also outside all the other disciplines and difficulties he and his mother lived with. Once on the pony's back he was so marvellously free that he forgot his own problems and even his mother's problems. He forgot the curious problem of his strange father, and the grip the town always seemed to have on him and his mother. In fact Eric simply forgot himself, so he didn't want to think about the money now. It was a wrong connection. Moreover, money for nothing always went to jodhpurs and riding boots, something he didn't resent but simply accepted as inevitable. And when he mentioned it to his mother and told her that it would be pretty good if he could win the five pounds, she told him, 'If you think of the money you'll only lose. It's always bad to think of money like that.'

'I know,' Eric said.

'You don't have to think about it,' his mother said again. 'It's wrong.' To Mrs Thompson, too, money came from work. Any other way of getting it was a fault which she didn't understand in the human system.

'Mr Hunt says he's got a course set up at Mr Miller's place,' Eric told her. 'He wants me to go down there and practise a bit.'

'You do as Mr Hunt says,' she told him. 'He's a kind man.'

'Dora thinks I might be able to win,' he went on, finishing off the piece of fried bread and dripping his mother had put on his plate.

'She's a nice girl, Dora. I wish there were a lot more like her,' Mrs Thompson said. 'You're lucky to have such good friends.'

'I suppose so,' Eric said slowly, because he still had not worked out what his friendship with Dora really meant to him.

His first problem was the blacksmith – Joe Hislop. Eric had often watched Mr Hislop shoeing horses, and had always admired the perfection of his black-handed skill – shaping hoofs and shoes and driving nails clean into the hoof without ever touching the frog, which was the sensitive flesh of the hoof. But when he went to Mr Hislop with the pony Mr Hislop was sceptical because Mr Hislop was a sceptical man.

'You don't need shoes on the pony unless you're going to ride him on asphalt or on hard ground,' he told Eric.

'I know,' Eric said, 'but Mr Hunt wants me to shoe him for the Agricultural Show.'

'I know what Bert Hunt wants. But once a horse is shod, Snow, he gets used to it and he ought to go on being shod and that costs money which you haven't got.'

'When I've finished with the Agricultural Show can't you just take the shoes off?'

'Not straight off. It's not a good idea. You've got to wait until the hoof starts growing again and hardening on the top.'

'Then I'll bring him here and you can take them off when the hoofs have grown,' Eric said.

'That's what you say, Eric, but what does Bert Hunt say?'

'He's my pony, Mr Hislop,' Eric pointed out.

'Then make sure he stays your pony,' Mr Hislop said. 'I doubt if your old man was thinking of the Agricultural Show when he gave you the pony. It wasn't his kettle of fish.'

Mr Hislop had known Eric's father since they were boys, and like his father Mr Hislop was an old man with a long face and a drooping grey moustache. Two fingers were missing from his left hand, lost, it was said, when Joe had been drunk one day at his forge. Instead of hammering nails into the hoofs of Mr Gerin's draft horse he had hammered off two of his fingers. In fact Mr Hislop didn't drink, was a strict Baptist, and had lost his fingers repairing a harvester.

Now, watching Mr Hislop cleaning and rasping the hoofs and shaping the shoes and spiking them and burning them into the horn, Eric wondered why it didn't hurt the pony.

'It's just a toe nail, like yours,' Mr Hislop said when Eric asked him. 'He doesn't feel it. But if I drive the nail into the frog he'll let me know.'

What had always impressed Eric most, and impressed him now with the pony, was that no matter how wild the horses were, how restless, once they were in Mr Hislop's hands they raised their hoofs obediently and let him cut and rasp and burn and nail. When he had finished the pony Mr Hislop took a brush with some blacking on it and blacked the hoofs.

'Come back the night before the Show and I'll check the shoes and give them a bit of fresh black,' he said. 'And don't forget. He's not going to be as light-footed as he was. And watch him when he trots. His feet will slide a bit at first.'

Once on the pony Eric felt it all, and so did the pony who now seemed to lift his legs a little higher and dig them in a little harder, so that Eric felt the jar on his backside. But the pony seemed to be pleased with the shoes, although Eric knew that he would never like them himself.

Thereafter, for the following weeks, Eric saddled and bridled the pony every day after school and rode him the back way around the town to Mr Miller's place where Mr Hunt had set up a meandering line of crates from his grocery store, as well as three jumps made of light poles resting on more crates.

Mr Hunt had shown him the route around the crates and the way to jump the poles, and as Eric rode around the course, time after time, he kept thinking that everything had become so different between him and the pony that he no longer knew what he was doing, nor did the pony. Whatever it was they just did it. But one day as he left Mr Miller's place and met Mr Richards on his stiff leg, the old soldier held the pony by the bridle and said in his abrupt way, 'I told you to forget about riding with a saddle.'

Eric hadn't seen Mr Richards for some time, and he felt himself blushing guiltily as Mr Richards looked at the pony's shod feet, and then looked sternly with his steel grey eyes at Eric himself.

'I know, Mr Richards,' Eric said, 'but Mr Hunt wants me to ride in the Agricultural Show, so he loaned me the saddle.'

'You were far better off without it,' Mr Richards said. 'You rode better, and the pony knew what you were doing.'

'Yes, I know,' was all Eric could manage.

'You ought to chuck it in,' Mr Richards said.

'I can't now,' Eric said. 'I've promised Mr Hunt.' He didn't say that he felt he owed something to Mr Hunt for all the trouble he had taken, but that was what he wanted to say.

'Never mind Hunt,' Mr Richards said. 'All that show riding is just show-off riding. It'll never make a horseman of you.'

'I know.'

'It's spoiling you and the pony.'

'I know,' Eric said, and now that Mr Richards had said it, and he himself had admitted it, Eric knew the true extent of the change in him and the pony.

'When I've finished with the Show,' he told Mr Richards, 'I'll give it up.'

'If I were you I'd give it up now.'

But Eric shook his head and said, 'I can't do that, Mr Richards. Not yet. It wouldn't be fair.'

'Well, I've told you,' Mr Richards said. 'You're taking the spirit out of him.'

It was true. These days the pony was almost always still. He was no longer restless or curious or spontaneous. He did what he did now – on his shod feet – with a deliberate and firm step but no real interest. Not like before. As if to restore a little of the old spirit, Mr Richards let go the bridle and slapped the pony hard on the rump so that he took off with some of his old verve.

That night Eric told his mother what Mr Richards had said, and he also tried to explain what was happening between him and the pony. But his mother listened and said, 'Until you got the saddle you were both like two wild things. And what was to become of you and the pony if you went on like that?'

'I don't know,' Eric said. 'But it was much better before.'

'Well I'm not sure what's better,' his mother said unhappily and began to clear the table.

Eric was thinking only of the pony and he didn't notice his mother's troubled and unhappy look. 'After the Show,' he said, 'I'll give Mr Hunt his saddle back.'

And having made the decision a second time Eric felt as if he had done something positive to restore whatever had been lost between himself and the pony, although it was not going to be quite like that at all.

Chapter 7

The Agricultural Show filled the town for two days with country people arriving in trucks, open tourers, gigs, buggies and on horseback. The Show took place on Friday and Saturday, and the entire school was given Friday off as well as the usual Saturday. There were, in fact, competitions for the local school children, who submitted best writing, essays, and a description of the town of St Helen. Girls competed with fine needlework, cushion covers, doyleys and even hand-kerchiefs.

Eric had received in the mail (the first letter he had ever received) the official entry certificate which allowed him this time to ride through the big wooden gate rather than crawl through a hole at the back. He had done the usual Saturday jobs on the Friday because his pony event was on the Satur-day. So his mother had put the iron on the stove the night before and freshly ironed his white shirt and navy-blue shorts, which he had not worn for some time, so that they were now tight on him.

'I didn't realize you'd grown so much even though Father O'Connel told me the other day,' his mother said when he put them on in the morning. 'And there's no time to let them out now.'

'They're all right,' Eric said although they felt as if they might split at any moment. Even his polished shoes, though well worn, were tight, and Eric noticed a strange look on his mother's face as she inspected him – ready for the Show.

'You must have shot up,' she said and gave him his lunch

of egg sandwiches and a piece of cake in a paper bag, which she put in a cloth bag to sling over his shoulder. 'I'll just have to make you a new pair of pants.'

That day Eric didn't run to the paddock. He walked there to make sure that he didn't get his shoes dusty. He gave old Dixie her usual feed, but Mr Hunt had told him not to feed the pony until the evening. 'They run better when they're a little empty,' he said. So Eric bridled and saddled the pony who stood quite still. Then he pulled himself up on the saddle which he had polished with a soft rag and a little boot polish, making it seem older rather than newer.

'I wish we weren't going,' he said unhappily to the pony as they left the paddock.

But the pony seemed to have adapted himself to the character he was now about to play. He trotted neatly on his freshly-blacked shoes and then cantered gently as Eric took him around the dirt roads to the Show Ground at the other end of the town.

Bob Anderson, who usually worked as a projectionist at the local cinema, was guarding the big wooden gates which were wide open. Bob stopped trucks and gigs as they came to the gate. He checked their tickets, or sent them to the ticket booth, and then waved them in with a commanding gesture.

'Well look at old Snow,' he said as Eric showed his official contestant's entry pass. 'All dressed up and somewhere to go at last. What are you entered for? The best dressed horse and rider?'

'No, the pony event,' Eric said seriously.

'In you go,' Bob said. 'And if you win the pony event I'll let you in free tomorrow.' It was Saturday, the last day of the Show, so there was no Show at all the next day. But Eric didn't feel like laughing at Bob's jokes.

Once inside the grounds, which were packed with people walking around the tents and inspecting the exhibits and visiting the side shows and watching the events in the arena, Eric didn't know where to go, nor did he feel like asking. So he rode as far out of the mess of tents and cars and parked lorries as he could, and without any kind of resistance or false shying from the pony. In fact, Eric hardly noticed the pony's good behaviour as he began to realize that he would never find the pony corral unless he rode closer to the arena, through the crowds and the exhibits.

'Eric . . .'

It was, to Eric, a cry from the wilderness. It was Dora Hunt.

'Over here,' she called.

He turned the pony in the direction of her voice, but he still couldn't see her. He had to pick his way through a crowd of people, some of whom he knew. Some of them greeted him with comments on his sudden transformation from barefoot boy to neat, black-shod rider.

'Eric, you look like a brand-new invention,' Mrs Cameron said to him, and though she meant it good-naturedly, Eric felt even more self-conscious of his appearance and his presence.

He found Dora by the roped-off pony corral. There were ten ponies tied to a rail, a small table for the contest officials, benches for the boys and girls who were riding, and some folding wooden chairs for the relatives of the contestants. In fact the place was full of children and parents drinking lemonade and kola beer and eating quartered oranges. At a glance Eric noticed that all the other children contestants were in jodhpurs, and most of them were attended by a father or a mother or some adult.

'You have to report to Mr Stone at the table,' Dora said.

Dora was dressed in a crisp cotton dress. She was wearing a soft straw hat with cherries on it, and her shoes were dustless. She even carried a little handbag, which to Eric made her seem years older than himself. In fact he was already aware that when he got off the pony he would be something of an exception here, so different in fact that he would stand out like a sore Australian thumb.

'Go on,' Dora said as she fondled the pony's nose affectionately and opened the rope gate. 'Go on in.'

Reluctantly Eric rode into the corral and found a place at the rail. He got off the pony, tied the bridle to the rail and then, aware that his cloth lunch bag was still slung over his chest, he hurriedly took it off and walked with Dora to the little table where the official, Mr Stone from the E.S. and A. Bank, was talking to one of the Fowler boys from the big wheat farm across the big river, near the Wakool.

'You get one of those rosettes,' Dora whispered to him.

'Hello, Snow,' Mr Stone said. 'We've been waiting for you to turn up.'

'Hello, Mr Stone,' Eric said. 'I couldn't find the way.'

'Never mind. You're here now. And I must say you look very smart.' Mr Stone knew what he was looking at, and Eric knew that Mr Stone was trying to put him at ease. 'Have you got your contestant's form?'

Eric had it in his cotton lunch bag, and he gave it to Mr Stone who unthinkingly sniffed it and said, 'You've obviously got some pretty good egg sandwiches in there, Eric.'

'That's right, Mr Stone.'

'Good. Because you'll have one elimination ride this morning and if you're lucky two for the final this afternoon. So just relax until your number is called, then you ride into the arena up to the judges' table and they'll tell you what to do. Nothing to it.'

Eric nodded.

'There's your rosette for your shirt, only don't pin it to your hairy flesh, will you,' Mr Stone said with a smile.

Dora laughed and nudged Eric who also laughed.

'What number is he, Mr Stone?' Dora asked.

'Four. So he'll be one of the first.'

Mr Stone gave Eric a number 4 painted on two cloth

patches with tie strings to them, and as they walked away Dora took the numbered patches and said: 'I'll tie them on for you.'

Eric knew that Dora was being very helpful, but he wished suddenly and rather sadly that she wouldn't be so helpful. Nonetheless he was glad she was here, because he didn't know any of the other boys to talk to. Only two of them were town boys, both a little older than he was: Jock Hay and Tom Littock. 'Whatcha, Eric,' Jock said. And Tom said, 'It's old Snow on his wild-west pony.'

Eric laughed nervously, and Dora whispered to him, 'You'll beat them easy. Tom sticks his elbows out, and Jock just bumps up and down.'

The other boys, country boys, and two girls, were very curious about Eric, and they inspected him frankly, as Eric inspected them.

'I've got to go,' Dora said. 'My father is waiting for me on the other side.'

'All right,' Eric said.

'Don't forget,' she said. 'You just ride into the arena when your number's called.'

'Don't worry. I won't forget.'

'I'll see you later,' she said.

'Taroo,' Eric said.

'Taroo,' she replied and left Eric standing with his lunch bag in his left hand, and with the right one trying to loosen his tight pants which he was now more frightened of. He warned himself not to sit down. Instead he walked back to the pony who was standing perfectly still in line with the other ponies, and he began to run his hand over the pony's flanks while secretly inspecting the others.

He knew already that not one of them was as well made and as perfect as his. And though their bridles and saddles were newer and brighter, his own little horse was a beauty, and Eric felt proud of him and knew that whatever he saw here, the

75

others must also see. In fact the real success or failure now depended on Eric himself in the saddle.

So he waited. And as the first number (Tom Littock) was called, Eric was suddenly aware that something immeasurable was facing him. He watched Tom trot his pony down the little corridor to the arena, which Eric had not yet seen. Then he waited, stiff and expectant, for Tom to return.

Number two was called, Stalky Skye, a country boy, as Tom rode back at a slow walk.

Again Eric waited.

Stalky returned, and then number three was called: Brigitte Malone from the big dairy farm along the river.

And as Brigitte eventually trotted back, hot and puffing, he heard 'Number four . . .'

Eric was aware of his lunch bag. He didn't want to put it down, so he slung it across his chest and pulled himself up on the saddle. He felt his trousers tighten uncomfortably as he rode down the little roped-in corridor towards the arena. It was about twenty yards long, and as the pony trotted happily towards the opening, Eric stared ahead, wondering what sort of exposure he was riding into.

When he reached the edge of the arena and saw the vast perimeter of the oval packed with people, he instinctively stopped the pony dead, and for a moment they just stood there. The pony, impatient to get on with his new role, strained forward. He wanted to go on. But Eric held him back, and without realizing it, without thinking about it, Eric knew that this was not for him. It was not a sudden lack of courage. He knew he could outride any of the others if he went in there, but he also knew, as he held himself on the very edge of the huge arena, that he was a barefoot Red Indian or he was nothing at all.

It was the pony who wanted to go on, but Eric suddenly and angrily pulled the pony's head right round, dug his two hard heels fiercely into the soft flanks not once but again and again, and then almost physically forced the pony to jump the little rope fence of the entrance corridor.

'Go on. Go on,' Eric shouted at the pony who seemed reluctant to leave the place.

But Eric's fierce kicking and slapping forced the pony into a gallop, so that they cut a swathe through the startled groups of people who scattered before them. And, finding a sudden hole in the busy throng, Eric had the pony galloping as he went out through the gates and disappeared down the dusty street.

He didn't stop until he reached the paddock, and it was only when he pulled the saddle off the pony that he remembered the five-pound prize he had abandoned.

'Oh, my God,' he said aloud, echoing his mother's usual cry of despair.

The saddle was still in his hand, and as he looked at it, and thought about it, he said miserably to himself, 'Well ... I wouldn't have won it anyway,' which didn't quite convince the salty tears that appeared on his cheeks before he could stop them. But they went away when he said with far more conviction, 'I didn't want to win anyway.'

Chapter 8

When Mrs Thompson asked Eric why he was back so soon and asked, 'What happened?' Eric said, 'Nothing, I didn't go in.'

'But you've still got your number on,' his mother pointed out.

Eric had forgotten the number and the rosette, and his lunch bag was still slung across his chest. 'I didn't want to do it,' he said. 'I wouldn't have won anyway, and the pony didn't like it.'

His mother looked at her son and knew that there were feelings and decisions going on which he couldn't explain, and possibly didn't understand. She was for ever facing her own decisions and her own lonely choices; but whatever she was in this town and in this house and in their life, so was her son.

'It doesn't matter,' she said to him. 'You couldn't help it.'

He wanted to say that he *could* help it, that he had done it deliberately. But there was so much to explain that he couldn't explain anything at all.

'Dora Hunt was there,' he said.

'Did you explain to Mr Hunt what happened?'

'I didn't see him,' Eric said.

'You'd better tell him first thing,' she said, 'so he doesn't think you just rode away.'

'I'll tell him next Saturday,' he said.

That seemed to worry Mrs Thompson. 'That's a whole week away,' she pointed out.

'I know. But I won't see him until then.'

Eric knew that he needed a week to think up something to say – to find courage enough to explain to Mr Hunt what had happened when in fact he had no real explanation at all. He also knew he would have to face the whole town and the school because everybody would know by Monday morning what he had done.

'Well, just so long as you thank him,' Mrs Thompson was saying.

Which left Eric trying to decide what to do now about the pony. There was still the rest of Saturday, but the old Saturday afternoon pleasures of disappearing into the countryside had been lost, and it seemed to Eric that he must somehow find out if they were lost forever.

'Can I have my lunch now?' he asked his mother as he took off the lunch bag.

'All right,' she said. She was sewing a white quilt for Mrs Cameron, and as Eric watched her tiny feet working the pedal of the sewing machine he noticed that she was bare-footed.

'You haven't got your slippers on,' he said.

'I've got to sew them up. They're coming to pieces,' she said. 'I haven't had time.' She got up. 'I'll put the kettle on for the tea, and you can eat the sandwiches.'

Eric said he would change his clothes, and as he stripped off his shirt and trousers and shoes and grey stockings, he knew that from now on he would only ride the pony bareback. No saddle, ever again. But when he had finished his lunch and was down at the paddock putting the bridle on the pony, there was a moment when Eric knew that the pony was waiting for the saddle to follow. When it didn't come the pony stood stock still when Eric leapt on his bare back, and though he did everything that would normally inspire an explosive take-off, the pony didn't respond at all and Eric shouted at him: 'Why don't you go? Go on ...' he shouted again as he dug in his heels.

The pony walked determinedly and stubbornly through

the gate, which Eric had learned to tie up without dismounting. In the happy days it was all done as the pony made tight little circles of impatience to be off. But today he waited patiently, and once again Eric had to dig his heels in.

'You're just being stubborn,' he said angrily.

And the pony went on being stubborn. Though Eric tried all the old bare-back manoeuvres and urging and secret noises, and though he tried himself to behave in the old way, the pony behaved as if he had a saddle on his back, which made Eric furious because he couldn't make the pony understand anything any more.

'You're doing it on purpose,' Eric protested.

But the pony persisted and trotted on neatly as if Eric was riding happily to the saddle, whereas Eric was bumping up and down uncomfortably on a bare back. For the rest of the afternoon the pony ignored all communication except the rather savage blows from Eric's bare heels. Finally, Eric took the pony across the bridge of the little river to the flat wide banks where they loved to gallop along the rather soft sand and pick their way in and out of the complicated little bumps and rises on the bank. But today the pony had no interest in the joys of the wide open space and at the end of the afternoon Eric doubted if he would ever get back the old relationship between them.

It was the same all week after school. Eric was teased about his plunging escape from the arena, but far less than he expected. The worst anyone said to him came from Mr Smythe, the new chemist, who said, 'I hear your pants split open, Snow, and you were left bare-arsed in front of all the little girls.'

'No, I wasn't,' Eric said indignantly.

'I was only joking,' Mr Smythe said. 'What happened anyway?'

'The pony bolted,' Eric said, which had become his

standard explanation and which most people decided to accept, including the teachers and pupils at school.

By keeping far away from the main street, coming and going to school, he didn't run into Mr Hunt, but he couldn't avoid Dora.

'Did he really bolt?' Dora asked him when they met briefly after school on the Monday.

'Yes. I mean he didn't like the show arena.'

'But he seemed so quiet.'

'You can never tell what he's thinking though,' Eric said knowingly.

'I don't suppose you can,' Dora agreed. 'And you would have won too.'

'I don't know about that,' Eric said, and then he said quickly, 'Tell your father I'll bring his saddle back on Saturday.'

'You don't have to,' she told him.

'I know. But it's better . . .' And he left Dora as quickly as he could while she was still shaking her head over him in a puzzled way.

By the end of the week Eric had won back nothing of the old way or the old contact even though he had persisted bareback. The pony insisted on behaving as a town pony, a saddle pony, and when Saturday morning came, and Eric saddled up for what he thought would be the last time, it was only too obvious that the pony was pleased to have the saddle on his back again. He stood still and seemed neat and proud and pleased, and as Eric pulled himself up on the saddle, the pony waited for a command to move.

'You're just showing off,' Eric said bitterly. Then he said, 'Just go. Go on.' He dug his bare heels into the pony's flanks and the pony trotted along the main street as if he was now on proud display to the entire world.

They arrived unseen at Mr Hunt's store, and while Eric

weighed Slash's potatoes he saw Mr Hunt coming and going, although he didn't say anything to Eric. But Eric knew it would come, and eventually Mr Hunt simply beckoned him outside with his finger.

'Well, young Snow Thompson,' Mr Hunt said. 'I hear the pony bolted on you.'

Eric knew he owed it to Mr Hunt to be truthful so he said, 'No, he didn't, Mr Hunt. It was me. I didn't want him to go in there.'

'Why not? What happened to you?'

'Nothing,' Eric said boldly. 'I didn't want to do it, that's all.'

Mr Hunt looked at Eric for a moment, and Eric felt that his bare legs and feet and worn trousers and shirt were being looked at very closely for some reason or other. But he found himself face-to-face with Mr Hunt without fear or shame.

Mr Hunt laughed. 'I guess you're just not a Show Rider, Snow. That's all there is to it. I shouldn't have tried to make you one.'

'It was the saddle,' Eric said.

'Why? What's the matter with it?'

'Nothing. Only it's not the way I was used to riding.'

Mr Hunt scratched his head for a moment and said, 'I wouldn't blame the saddle if I were you. Too easy. In fact it's never what you put on a horse, but the way you ride it that counts.'

'Anyway, I brought it back,' Eric said. 'I left it on the fruit box.' He had put it back, nose down on the box the way he had first found it.

Mr Hunt glanced at the saddle. 'That's a pity,' he said, 'because I wanted you to do some real riding with me tomorrow. Not this public Show Grounds stuff, but the sort of thing horses are made for. But I wouldn't let you do it without a saddle. Too dangerous.'

Eric didn't understand. 'I don't know what you mean,' he said.

'Well I'll tell you what I've been thinking, Snow – I've been thinking that you took one look at that Show Grounds arena, and said it wasn't your cup of tea. Am I right?'

Eric nodded. 'I suppose so,' he said.

Mr Hunt went on, 'So I thought the best thing to do was to take you with me over to the Riverain tomorrow when we will be helping the Eyre stockmen round up their Welsh ponies from the bush.' Mr Hunt dropped a friendly hand on Eric's shoulder as he continued in his amused, ever amused way. 'I thought that if we did that it would make up for my stupidity – trying to make you into something you're not. You're just like your old man, and I can't imagine him riding in a Show contest.' Mr Hunt laughed. 'So how about it? Just to make it up to me and Dora. As a favour.'

Eric had never thought of blaming Mr Hunt for what had happened, and to hear Mr Hunt cheerfully blaming himself now and asking, actually asking a favour, was very surprising and confusing.

'Well I can't say,' Eric told him. 'I'd have to ask my mother.'

'She'll agree, as long as you use the saddle. You can't ride Red Indian style in the bush – not when you're rounding up wild unbroken ponies. It's too dangerous.'

'I suppose so,' Eric said, but he had to resist. 'Mr Richards says I ought to ride bare-back, because I won't always have a saddle.'

Mr Hunt laughed again. 'You never know, Snow. You never really know, do you? Anyway, why don't you give it a final go. Do or die. All or nothing. You're a real Aussie, so it's worth a try.'

Eric again felt trapped by gratitude. Like his mother he knew instinctively that a kindness was also a persuasion, so reluctantly he agreed. 'Won't it take all day,' he said, 'if we're going over to the Riverain?'

'You're dead right. You'll have to meet me on the bridge

83

at eight o'clock. But don't bring any lunch with you. We'll boil the billy with the stockmen. Tell your mum we'll be back at about seven o'clock. And wear your shoes and socks. You don't want to cut your legs to pieces in the bush.'

'Okay,' Eric said (a word which had just arrived at school because some of the boys who had been on holiday in Melbourne had seen the first talkies).

So once again he took the saddle from the fruit box and threw it over the obedient and placid pony. Eric pulled himself up on the saddle slowly and even tolerated the pony's polite walk homewards. But he couldn't stand it for long. Suddenly he dug his heels in hard and the pony cantered. Then Eric forced him to gallop, saying as he leaned forward on the pony's neck: 'You'll get over it. You'll see.'

The next morning, early, his mother gave him a soft canvas smock as he was about to leave. The Mallee sky, normally clear and sunny, was autumnal and dry and peculiar, as if there was something threatening in the yellowish air. 'It's going to blow up a dust storm,' she said to him, 'and if it rains afterwards you'll get wet.'

A Mallee dust storm was something that everyone dreaded. For many years the Mallee wheat farmers had been cutting down the Mallee scrub to extend their wheat fields. But the scrub held the soil together, so that when it was removed the top soil was simply picked up and blown away in huge dark clouds by the sharp autumn winds that could follow the hot dry summers. Usually, the dust was so thick that it resembled a London fog – with high winds added. Sometimes it was a one day storm, sometimes it lasted two or three days, and the one hope of relief was that often these storms seemed to create a rival storm bringing even higher winds with dramatic lightning, thunder, dark clouds and torrential rain.

'But it'll be too hot to wear,' Eric protested, taking the smock.

'Then tie it around your waist, just in case.'

84

He accepted it as a rare instruction from his mother and said goodbye to her and walked to the paddock feeling for some strange reason that today was going to be an unpredictable sort of day for him and the pony.

He had already fed the pony and Dixie, and as he rode through the main street so early on a quiet Sunday morning the sound of the pony's steel-shod hoofs on the hard road seemed to Eric to belong to someone else, not to him and the pony.

'Good on you,' Mr Hunt said when Eric arrived on the bridge. 'Dead on time.'

Eric was surprised to see Dora. Dora on a bicycle, which she had lately been riding to school. ('Because my father says if I can ride a bike it'll be good practice for riding a pony.') Seeing her on the bike now Eric wondered why her father had not yet bought her a pony. The last time Eric had asked her about it she had said, 'My mother says I ought to wait until the right one comes along.'

'Is your father going to buy one of the Eyres' ponies today?' he asked her now.

'I don't know. But he's always wanted one for me.'

'Maybe that's what he's doing today.'

'You can't tell with Dad,' Dora said. 'He's like your pony: you never really know what he's up to. That's what my mother says.'

They were talking while Mr Hunt was discussing the weather (the hot, still air, the dull sky) with Sergeant Collins, the policeman, who usually fished the rising river early on Sunday morning. 'You'll be all right if the wind doesn't pick up,' Sergeant Collins was saying. 'Otherwise you're in for a bit of a duster.'

'You can't tell at this time of the year,' Mr Hunt said. 'It may be rain on the way.' He turned to Eric then and said, 'Are you ready, son?'

Eric mounted and said goodbye to Dora and followed Mr

Hunt across the bridge of the big river into New South Wales.

The country here was different, instantly. It was a vast pastoral plain – flat, open and empty. It was timbered grazing land, not farming land, and the dirt road went on and on to distant towns in New South Wales. But after six miles there was a timbered turn off to the Riverain Station which stocked both beef-cattle and sheep and enclosed two hundred thousand acres. The Welsh ponies which they were looking for usually grazed along the river, where there was bush and wet lands which acted as a sort of barrier that kept the ponies close to the river, because they didn't like the swampy ground.

As they turned off towards the Riverain, Eric and Mr Hunt rode side by side, sometimes walking sometimes trotting. But the pony often had to canter when Mr Hunt on his big black horse moved along at a leisurely trot. They didn't talk, and Eric knew he was riding in a different way now. He had never ridden beside another rider before and because they were both on their way to do something that was, after all, work, Eric felt happy on the saddle for the first time.

It took them over an hour to reach the Riverain Station, and when he rode up the long drive between the patient, drooping eucalypts to the big house, Eric knew he was entering a different kind of world. In fact this was a little world to itself: a white, low, graceful house, rich gardens, woolsheds, horses for the stockmen, and white painted rails around the horse paddock. When they went behind the house Eric saw stables and storehouses and a blacksmith's forge. Here the stockmen were already waiting with languid horses already saddled.

Eric dismounted, and holding the pony by the reins he squatted on a neat grass verge (dry now) while the men talked almost monosyllabically with Mr Hunt who eventually said, pointing to Eric, waiting by his pony, 'This is Andy Thompson's son, and he sticks to his horse like his old man.'

Eric was aware of friendly looks and a nod or two from the four stockmen, who looked like old men wearing old hats, not young men like Mr Hunt. There was more talk, and a lot of discussion about the weather. They pointed here and there and planned their operation before the four stockmen and Mr Hunt and Eric finally moved off, heading for the river which was outlined in the distance by thick gum trees.

'Stick by me as much as you can,' Mr Hunt said as they followed the stockmen at a walk, which to the pony meant a broken trot or an amble in order to keep up. 'And if we have to move fast, keep your eyes on the rabbit warrens and the ditches. There's a lot of them near the river. So watch out. But first of all we'll head for A.M.'s camp.'

Eric was suddenly happy. Even the pony seemed happy and at ease among his companions. There were no streets now. No Show Grounds. No showing off. It was straightforward riding, and though Eric wasn't told what they would do when they got to the bush, he was glad simply to go along with the others. He knew about rabbit warrens and ditches, even more than Mr Hunt, because in the Red Indian days it had become an instinct with pony and rider to avoid them, so he wasn't worried. At the end of another hour, walking and trotting, they had reached the bush, and once under the canopy of huge gum trees, padding softly on the dry-leafed surface, they sometimes rode single file until they came to a wagon and some feeding horses and two more men sitting near a fire which had a stake across the top. Two blackened billy cans were hanging from it, boiling, and under the billies, on the hot fire, meat was grilling in a large wire frame.

'A.M.'s old camp,' Mr Hunt told Eric.

'Tea up,' someone said as they dismounted and tied their horses to a worn bridle pole, or to the wheels of the wagon among loose uncut hay and water buckets.

Eric followed Mr Hunt and hooked his bridle over what

seemed at first to be a hitching post, but was in fact a very old wooden cross, and Eric saw that it was carved with worn, almost illegible writing, which said:

Here A.M. was bitten by a tiger snake and died,
March 3, 1881. A.M. died, not the snake.

'Poor old A.M., whoever he was,' Mr Hunt said to Eric, 'but you have to watch out for snakes around here. Particularly on a day like this. They haven't gone under for the winter, so they coil up in the open sometimes for a last bit of warmth.'

Eric knew that, so he simply nodded. He sat down near the wagon and listened and waited as one of the old men (Ben) at the fire handed out meat and home-made bread (from the Station) and mugs of tea. The men talked about the bush fire which had swept through part of the Riverain in the summer and killed two ponies and some sheep, and when Ben gave him his portion of meat and bread and sweet hot tea in a tin mug Eric ate hungrily so that he was finished before the others, who took their time about everything: eating, talking, riding, moving. They seemed to lean against the world, and Eric suddenly realized that his father was like these men. This was probably what he did all day and every day in the vast, empty country somewhere to the north. But instead of being fixed and living in the little houses behind the big house of the Riverain, like these men, his father would be forever on the move, living in the open like this as he followed a big herd of sheep or cattle, always looking for better pastures or taking the stock hundreds of miles to a market town or a railhead. Endless riding, and almost no other life at all.

'All right, Snow?' Mr Hunt asked him when they had finished. They mounted up again. 'Now I'll tell you what we're going to do,' Mr Hunt said. 'You and I will go with Bluey along the river, and when we see a pony we bring him in with whatever others we have. Above all we have to keep them ahead of us. If you see one back-track on Bluey and me, you ride off and herd him in. We can't use dogs on wild ponies because they're not like beef or sheep – they move too fast. So if one tries to back-track on us don't let him get away. Go after him. Have you got it?'

'Yes, I think so.'

'And keep your eye on Bluey and me.' Mr Hunt looked at the sky again. The sky was now darkening in the north and it was obvious that somewhere in the distance one of the Mallee dust storms was on the way. 'It looks like it's going to be a duster,' Mr Hunt said. 'But that won't hurt you as long as you keep us in sight.'

'Don't worry,' Eric said. 'I'll be all right.'

'Off we go then.'

The bush along the river was not all tall gums. Sometimes it was broken up by thick scrub or young trees, and when they reached the edge of the wetland there were huge ghost gums and sudden clumps of stark dead trunks in soft watery patches of ground. Somewhere here they came to the first two ponies, lying in the warm sand in a bend of the river, and they leapt up when Bluey shouted some queer word at them. They tried at first to break back behind the riders, but Bluey (a tiny unshaven man with a hat that looked as if it had been chewed around the edges by mice) – Bluey whistled and shouted, and they turned and trotted on ahead. Eric had seen some of these golden Welsh ponies in the stockyards when they were being shipped to Melbourne, and he thought they were the most beautiful ponies he had ever seen – barring his own. The Riverain stockmen usually called them Taffies, though sometimes they also called them Welshmen.

'How many Taffies are there?' Eric managed to ask Mr Hunt as they followed the two ponies.

'About thirty or forty,' Mr Hunt said.

'What does he do with them all?'

'Sells them, all over the country. The finest ponies in Australia – all young thoroughbreds, and bred wild the way they should be.'

It was almost another hour before Eric, lagging a little, spotted a Taffie which was trying to back-track (they now had six) and he turned his pony's head and cantered towards the wild little pony which was facing him as if waiting for him. Seeing Eric approach, he suddenly turned, lifted his head, and galloped deeper into the scrub and the bush. At almost the same time Eric felt the first puff of wind and he realized that the very air had thickened all around him, and he knew that the entire countryside would soon be smothered in a thick, rolling, blinding dust on the crest of a steady, harsh wind. So he tied his handkerchief (a cut up sheet) around his neck so that when the dust arrived he could pull it up over his mouth and nose. And like that he began to chase the shaggy golden Taffie.

It was rough ground; swampy on one side and bush on the other, and from the outset Eric's pony, who had so far done nothing more than follow the other riders, resisted any idea of plunging flat out after the fleeing Taffie.

'You're too slow,' Eric shouted at the pony as he saw the Taffie disappearing into the scrub. 'We'll lose him.'

But the pony would not flatten his ears and abandon his caution. He did not, as he normally did, try to find his own way between scrub, trees, pot holes and old logs, but left it to Eric to steer him one way or the other. It seemed as if he was deliberately cutting himself off from all communication with Eric.

But Eric persisted, and when the little Taffie was finally cornered against the swamp Eric had to dig in his heels and slap his hands on his pony's neck and force him to plunge across some soggy ground in order to drive the defiant Taffie forward.

It succeeded, but instead of it being natural, as it once

might have been to both pony and rider, it was now hard work for Eric to get the pony to do what he wanted done.

'What are you afraid of?' Eric said angrily to the pony. 'You're not going to break a leg.'

The pony kept his head down, as if he wanted nothing to do with any of this wild riding, and when the wind suddenly gusted and the first stinging blanket of dust hit them, the pony turned his head towards Eric as if to demand how long this was going to go on for.

'You're going to get a bit dusty,' Eric said. 'That's all.'

But it wasn't all.

Every time Eric tried to catch one of the strays that had back-tracked on Mr Hunt and Bluey, the pony refused to respond, and Eric had to call out to Mr Hunt that one of the Taffies was getting away, even as the air itself now began to fill with biting, swirling, pressing dust.

'After him then,' Mr Hunt shouted.

'The pony keeps baulking,' Eric said, 'and I can't catch up with them.'

'All right. All right,' Mr Hunt said and turned his big stallion to chase the escaping Taffie, which left Eric ashamed for himself and his pony.

In fact it wasted time. And the wind and the dust were now rolling over them and around them at full blast, as if the atmosphere itself had to be replaced by the reddish stinging earth which was already filling Eric's clothes and hair, and was making his eyes water. He pulled the handkerchief up over his nose and mouth and peered ahead, because he couldn't see much further than Mr Hunt, who was only twenty yards away. As they slowed to barely a walk, trying to keep their mounts aware of what they were doing in this rather purplish gloom, Eric knew that it would be all he could do to keep the others in sight.

'We're going to be late,' Mr Hunt shouted at Eric as he loomed up from nowhere, 'so never mind chasing any of the strays that get around us. Just leave them and stick close to me.'

The sky had now disappeared, and the pony reacted to this change in air and atmosphere by pulling hard on the reins, stretching his neck and flattening his ears, which was what he usually did when he didn't like something and was going to act accordingly.

'There's nothing to worry about,' Eric shouted at him above the wind as he reined the pony back for a moment. 'Just don't get nervous.'

But Eric felt the pony quivering, and when the next sudden press of wind and dust flew straight into their eyes and ears (and Eric could feel it now between the toes in his shoes and between his fingers which were sweating on the reins) he felt all the tensions that the pony felt.

'We're going to finish this in darkness, Snow,' Mr Hunt said, riding back on his pawing beast which was also nervous and blinded, so that Mr Hunt had to speak urgently and hastily through the bandanna around his face. 'Do you think you can do it?'

'I'm all right,' Eric said, although he could feel the pony trying to pull himself free by swinging his head from side to side in order to get the bit in his teeth, even though they were barely moving.

'Just keep close. We've done quite a big circle, and sooner or later we'll end up on A.M.'s old camp site, then we'll make a straight run to the Station. But it'll be dark by then, so watch out for those ditches.'

They were all in a hurry now, but they had to stop from time to time to avoid the dust, trying to brace themselves against it, and it seemed to Eric that they were hours struggling behind nothing. His own struggle was always with the pony who now began to shy seriously at any dim shape that loomed out of the murk: trees, logs, shadows, so that Eric was in danger of coming off.

'You're just going mad,' Eric shouted again above the wind as the pony reared on his hind legs at the figure of Mr Hunt passing. 'It's only Mr Hunt . . .' He struggled to hold the pony straight, instead of the curious, crab-like walk he was now adopting.

The pony responded to Eric's firm grip by trying to break from a walk into a canter, and then into a gallop, and it was only by leaning back as far as he could in the stirrups with a short rein tightened as hard as he could on the pony's mouth that Eric managed to hold him.

'Are you all right?' Mr Hunt called out as he passed hurriedly and nervously.

'I'm all right so far,' Eric shouted back, although he was no longer sure of the pony.

A moment later the pony finally got his head, leapt a small log, raced for what looked like an open space and at the last moment stopped so suddenly on his slightly bent front legs that Eric left the saddle and went over his head.

He felt the scrub catch his arms and his clothes and his face as he landed, and from long habit which was an instinct by now he didn't let go the reins. He hung on as the pony tried to back off, and with a speed that surprised Eric himself he was up on the pony's back before the pony could get away.

In the bare-back days a manoeuvre like that would have been a sporting contest between them, but Eric knew that this time the pony meant it and his steel-shod hoofs helped him do it because they dug in. In fact the pony had devised a new way of getting rid of Eric, and though Eric was alert the pony threw him twice more in the gathering darkness before they reached A.M.'s old camp.

There, Mr Hunt managed to get a look at Eric as a flash of lightning now lit the sky, and he said, 'Jesus Christ, Snow. What happened to you?'

Eric couldn't see what Mr Hunt saw, but he knew he was torn and bleeding from a dozen scratches. 'The pony threw me into the scrub,' he said as he tried to keep the pony still.

The other stockmen were now milling about the old camp site where there was a lot of panicky movement. The wagon was already on the move and Bluey shouted, 'For Christ's sake, Mr Hunt, hurry up. We're in for a real soaking when this blows out.'

In fact the wind had lulled, though the dust was still thick in the air, and even the horses could feel that something else was on the way. Thunder clouds were darkening the already dark sky, and with the first long roll of thunder the real threat of what was about to come out of the sky was felt by everybody.

'Do you want to ride the rest of the way on the wagon?' Mr Hunt asked Eric.

'No, I can get there,' Eric shouted.

'Well keep the wagon in sight,' Mr Hunt's voice said, 'and I'll keep an eye on you from time to time.'

'Okay,' Eric shouted back as cheerfully as he could.

He knew he was not frightened, and now that he caught glimpses of the whole herd of Taffies more or less bunched together, though still unpredictable, he suddenly felt secure despite the lightning. Whereas the pony was now in such a state of tension that he was turning circles on himself as he tried to break away with every flash and every crack of thunder.

It was now almost completely dark, and after a violent streak of lightning which cut the whole sky in two and was followed by an avalanche of thunder, the pony reared up on his hind legs and pawed the air. Eric hung on, but at the same moment it began to rain in the local measure of buckets full. It was so heavy instantly, that for a moment it literally dampened the pony's movement and it was almost impossible to keep the wagon in sight, even from a few yards. Occasionally Eric did see the spread of men and horses somewhere ahead, moving as if they too were literally flattened by the rain, but Eric knew that he was on his own now because the rain was a prelude to a new kind of anarchic wind which seemed to come from all directions. In one startling gush that slashed the heavy rain into Eric's face and into the pony's eyes it brought disorder to the darkness and the pony stretched his neck, got the better of Eric for just a moment, and then bolted into the void ahead.

Eric tried to hold him, but he knew it was impossible so he simply let the pony go, and in a moment he had passed Mr Hunt and some of the stockmen and was in among the Taffies where the pony stopped dead on his steel hoofs and Eric flew like a bird over his head.

Again Eric held the reins, and once again, even among the panicking Taffies, he was back on the pony before the pony knew what to do next.

'Are you there, Eric?' he heard Mr Hunt shout from somewhere. 'Are you okay?'

'Yes,' Eric managed as he wrestled with the wet pony again.

'Go back to the wagon,' Mr Hunt said. 'Keep out of the way of the Taffies, or you'll stampede them.'

Eric didn't try to answer but struggled to turn the pony back, which he did by sheer force, and he reached the wagon as a ball of lightning seemed to bounce off the trees ahead, and the thunder was so close overhead that it seemed to be falling on them.

'Get on if you like,' old Mr Dickinson, the wagoner, said to him. 'Tie him up behind.'

'Not me . . .' Eric said grimly because now he knew it was a real struggle between him and the pony; not a sporting one but a final all or nothing confrontation with a pony who had long since ceased to be a Red Indian, who no longer felt as Eric felt or wanted what Eric wanted, but simply wanted him off, whereas Eric was the rider who was determined to stay on. And because all talk and contact between them was now gone, and as Eric turned once more to ruthlessly reining the pony back to the speed of the Taffies and the wagon, he knew it was only a matter of time before the pony got his head again, which he did when the ditches began.

They were not really ditches but sudden hollows, which were not bad if they could be seen. But in the darkness, and under the cracking sky and the blundering wind and rain they were invisible pitfalls. The pony almost came down in one of them, and as he recovered his stride he finally got his head again and was off at full gallop.

This time Eric knew it was dangerous because of the ditches, so he tried to hold the pony. But the pony had his head down and Eric had to resort to something he had never done before – sawing the bit from one side to the other, which he knew would hurt the pony's mouth. But even this did not stop him, and Eric was aware that they were now bolting far away across the open plain into the empty darkness – away from the others, almost at a right angle. He sawed the bit again and again and, finally feeling it, the pony stopped short suddenly and angrily as they came in and out of a ditch, and Eric went off.

This time he knew he was hurt, but he still held the reins, and though he was shouting angrily at the pony and holding him, he couldn't leap on his back but had to grasp the stirrup and somehow get back on the saddle. When he was back on, the pony took off again and Eric knew that this time it was almost impossible to stop him because the pony kept stretching his neck until at last he got the bit in his teeth and Eric had no more control over him at all.

He didn't know how long they went on like that across the plain, into the wind, into the darkness, into the rain, with lightning occasionally showing them nothing but emptiness. But he knew that all he could do now was to hang on and wait for the pony to exhaust himself. But instead of that happening, the pony saw something that Eric didn't see – a snake, a log, or the remnant of an old fence, and taking the opportunity and using his steel–clad hoofs the way he had learned to use them he dug in his front legs and Eric flew off him again. But this time the girth of the saddle snapped and the saddle went off with him.

Even as he sailed through the air Eric felt that the pony had not only thrown him and rejected him, but had finally abandoned him, and he was feeling very bitter about it when he hit the ground and met nothing there but complete oblivion.

Chapter 9

Eric woke up in an iron bed in a tiny, rather dark room which was not his own. Expecting to be filthy and wet and muddy he was surprised to find himself in clean, coarse sheets, and wearing some kind of nightshirt. He didn't know where he was, and remembering his last flight through the air over the pony's head he realized that he must have been knocked out. Even without moving he discovered that his left arm was bandaged, that his face was sore, particularly his nose, and that he couldn't move his left leg, which seemed to be tied to the bed.

'I must have broken something,' he told himself dazedly, and suddenly remembering previous moments of confused darkness and people he went off to sleep as if there were no answers worth bothering about at the moment.

When he awakened again he saw an elderly woman with grey hair and a worn, sunburnt face bending over him, her pale blue eyes screwed up as if she was staring into the sun.

'So you finally decided to wake up,' she said to him. 'You're a sleeper, you are.'

Trying to work out where he was he said to her, 'Are you old Mrs Hunt?' Dora had a grandmother who was rarely seen, and Eric thought for a moment that he was lying in the Hunts' house.

'No, I'm not that one,' she said. 'I'm old Mrs Dickinson, Ben's wife. The one with the wagon. You're in our house on the Riverain.'

'What happened to the pony?' he said weakly.

'They caught him yesterday, and Mr Hunt took him home.'

'Is he hurt?'

'Yes, but they don't know yet if it's bad or not. You must lie quiet. You've had concussion.'

'Is it still Sunday?' Eric said.

'No. It's Tuesday.'

'Then how did I get here?' Eric asked, finally aware enough to be surprised.

'They spent half the night looking for you. Then Ben found you in a ditch and brought you here in the wagon. So be quiet now. You can talk later.'

But Eric persisted. 'What's the matter with my leg?'

'It's broken. The doctor was here yesterday. You were in a delirium, shouting at everybody, so he put you to sleep and he put your leg in splints. Do you want something to drink?'

'I don't know,' Eric said. 'I ought to get up now.'

Mrs Dickinson's old face seemed to unfold itself as if a smile was something so rare among the lines and sadness of her watery blue eyes that Eric thought she was going to cry. But she laughed and held her hand in front of her mouth, though not before Eric had seen that she only had two front teeth. 'You'd fall flat on your face if you tried to get out of that bed,' she said. 'So don't try.'

'My mother doesn't know where I am,' he said.

'Yes she does. She came out yesterday with Doctor Legge.'

'Well ... I ought to go home,' he said trying to sit up.

'Not yet. You just lie there now, and I'll get you a cup of tea. But don't try to get out of bed,' she ordered in her harsh though friendly voice.

'All right,' Eric said resignedly. 'But I'm not thirsty.'

'Tea won't hurt you,' she told him.

Thereafter, Eric lived in a strange unknown world in which unknown stockmen and unknown women and even the Eyres and their crippled daughter, Josie, came to see him. They all told him he would be up and about in no time, and when

Doctor Legge also came to see him Eric remembered the little doctor who usually drove an open Chrysler and always waved to him with a bandaged thumb in the air. He was a small man with a grey drooping moustache and friendly eyes, and he told Eric he was lucky to be alive.

'If the saddle hadn't come off, and if your feet had caught in the stirrups, you would have been dragged, and that would have been the end of you. So you were lucky that you were thrown clean with the broken saddle and only broke your leg and got a few scratches and bruises and a bit of concussion. How's your head now?' Doctor Legge asked him.

'All right,' Eric said. He was sitting up and feeling almost normal.

The doctor made him hold out his hands, felt his fingers, inspected his eyes, made him move his head and cough, and then asked him to listen to his watch.

'You're as fit as a fiddle,' Doctor Legge said, 'and you can go home to your own bed tomorrow. Your mother is waiting for you.'

'Where are my clothes?'

'Never mind your clothes now. You'll be flat on your back with your leg for some time.'

Eric had one last question of Dr Legge. 'Is it going to cost a lot of money, Dr Legge?'

'Broken legs always come free with me, Eric, because my name is Legge. Never charge for a broken leg.'

The next day Mr Hunt came in his car to take Eric home, and when he came into the room Eric was eating a mutton chop with tomato sauce on it. Mr Hunt looked at it and pulled a face and said: 'You looked just like that piece of meat with tomato sauce on it when we found you. You were a very bloody looking sight, I can tell you.'

'From my arm?' Eric said.

'No. From your nose. It was bleeding all over the place. Have you seen your face lately?'

'No.'

'Well don't look at it for a while. It'd frighten a monkey's uncle.'

'Where's the pony, Mr Hunt?'

'I took him back to the paddock with Dixie.'

'Is he all right?'

'We think so,' Mr Hunt said. 'But something's wrong with his front legs. Mr Taylor, the vet, thinks he probably strained the tendons, and he's got a cut under his belly which he probably got when the saddle came off.'

'It broke when he threw me off,' Eric said. 'It just broke.'

'It wasn't your fault, old son. It was an old saddle, and the girth probably got damp and it stretched. The stitching must have been rotten. I chucked the whole thing in the river on the way home. But we're pretty proud of you after that ride. How many times did he throw you off?'

'I don't know. About ten.'

'Well, you stuck it out, that's the main thing, and the pony didn't.'

'He was different, Mr Hunt,' Eric said. 'The saddle made him different.'

'You tamed him, that's why he's different. But he was obviously scared stiff. So was my stallion. And so was I. And I suppose you were yourself.'

'No I wasn't,' Eric said truthfully. 'I wasn't frightened at all.'

Mr Hunt looked at him and saw something he hadn't seen before. 'No, I don't believe you were, son. They all think you did pretty good.'

When Mr Hunt and Bluey carried him out to Mr Hunt's car, some of the other stockmen, wives, children, and even Josie Eyre were there to see him off, and he knew as he left the Riverain that he didn't feel the same any more. And he went on feeling different when he arrived home and was left helpless on his bed, while his mother fussed a little but then became curiously quiet and sometimes sat by his bed for half an hour at a time without saying anything.

It took another five weeks before he was on one leg and crutches, and in that time his mother did not tell him how she had felt when Mr Hunt had arrived in the middle of the night to say that her son was hurt; nor did she tell him that for a moment her whole life had simply stopped. If anything she seemed now to be a little sterner and firmer with him which he accepted almost gladly, because he knew he had caused her a lot of unhappiness and trouble.

So they didn't say anything to each other about what had happened or about the pony, except once when he asked her who was feeding Dixie and the pony. 'Never mind about that,' she said. 'Mr Richards is doing it himself.'

But the day came when he was able to hobble out on his crutches (supplied by Slash, who had made them out of two old brooms) and swing himself down to the paddock.

'I'm just going down to see the pony,' he said to his mother.

Mrs Thompson nodded but didn't say anything.

It was early morning, and though he had been thinking of the pony and wondering what he would do now that there was nothing left of the Red Indian, he looked forward nonetheless to seeing the pony, almost hoping he would get one of the old, affectionate nuzzles.

When he reached the paddock he could see Dixie eating the last of the chaff in the slippery bin, but when he looked around the paddock he couldn't see the pony anywhere, and he realized that he wasn't there.

The pony had gone.

All the way back to the house on his crutches he puzzled about it because his mother had said nothing about the pony not being there. When he swung himself into the kitchen and said to her, 'What happened to the pony? He's not there,' she sat down on a chair at the kitchen table and said, 'He's gone to Mr Hunt.'

'What for? I thought he was all right.'

'He's gone for good, Eric,' his mother said.

'Why? What was the matter with him?'

'Nothing,' she said, and she told Eric to sit down, and after a long time when she seemed to be wondering how to tell him something, Mrs Thompson said, 'I had to give him to Mr Hunt, because I owed him ten pounds, eleven and sixpence ...'

She stopped suddenly, and Eric heard but didn't understand.

Then Mrs Thompson rushed on with tumbling words as if everything had to be said in one sudden miserable burst, 'It wasn't right, Eric, because when your father came home last time he took all the money I had to pay for what he had spent on the pony and a new stock horse for himself, and I already owed Mr Hunt eight pounds then, and I was paying it off a little at a time but I couldn't pay it all,' she said, tangling up her hands now as she waited for Eric to say something.

Eric knew that she wanted him to say something, but he didn't know what to say. She had been talking with her eyes cast down, and now when she suddenly looked up at him he saw the real pain in her tiny face.

'All the money I get now goes to the rent and light and wood and the cloth I sew up,' she went on, still tangling her hands as she tangled her words. 'Mrs Cameron hasn't paid me for the cloth and the quilts, and Mrs Flynn hasn't paid me for the work I did for her. Nobody pays me when I've finished, so I didn't have any money at all and I couldn't go on getting groceries, eggs and butter and potatoes and flour and things like that without paying for them. I couldn't do it any more, Eric. It was wrong, and I don't know where it would have ended. It was all wrong ...'

Eric managed to say, 'I know it was, Mum ...'

'So Mr Hunt's given me five pounds more in credit as well

as settling the bill, so I *had* to do it. I didn't want to take the pony away, Eric, but I didn't know what else to do. I didn't know how to tell you what I'd done, so I thought I'd wait until you'd found out for yourself that the pony had gone.'

It seemed to Eric that everything his mother was saying, though a complete and stunning surprise, was nonetheless the expected and predictable end to his possession of the pony. But he saw too that his normally good-natured and never-glum mother was in tears, which was so rare that Eric didn't know what to do. He only knew that he didn't want to see her like this.

'It's all right about the pony . . . it's all right . . . it's all right,' he said quickly, because he didn't know what else to say and he didn't want her to see him upset.

He watched his mother carefully wiping away her very wet tears with the tea cloth she was holding. 'When you were hurt,' she said, 'I thought it was not right, it just wasn't right. I didn't want you to grow up like your poor father. He doesn't know what else to do. But that wasn't why I gave Mr Hunt the pony,' she said hurriedly, as if she had to explain it to herself. 'It was the groceries . . .'

But Eric remembered Mr Hunt's promise not to buy the pony, and Dora's as well, and he said, 'What did Mr Hunt say?'

'He said he didn't want the pony. He said it was yours, and you ought to keep it. And Dora stopped me in the street and said she wouldn't ride it. But I told them that I'd sell the pony to someone else if they didn't take it, and give them the money, and that if anybody had to have the pony you wanted them to have it. Isn't that right?'

Eric nodded as the truth of his mother's desperate words now began to dawn on him.

'I had to do it, Eric,' his mother said miserably again. 'I just don't want you to grow up like your father. He's hardly a human being any more. Nobody understands what I mean, only Father O'Connel understands, and he said I was doing the right thing. You don't want to be like your father, do you? You don't want to do what he does. You can't be like that. You've got to be something else, Eric. Do you know what I mean?'

Eric finally understood. 'Yes, I know what you mean, Mum,' he said, because he realized now what she had been struggling so hard to tell him.

She knew that when he ran down to the paddock and jumped on the pony and disappeared into the bush he was simply freeing himself wildly from everything around him: from the town and its people, from his bare-footed life, and even from Mrs Thompson herself. Like his father, he was learning to lose himself in the emptiness of the vast Australian horizon. And she also knew that if he kept the pony, if he had it once more, he would somehow win it back to the old ways, and once again they would be Red Indians in the wilderness, because that was the only way that he and the pony could live together.

'Don't worry any more,' he said to her. 'I don't want to ride him again. Something went wrong with him anyway. He wasn't the same. I didn't like him any more. Not after the saddle. So you don't have to worry about it . . . not any more.'

They couldn't talk at all, either of them, for a moment.

'Mr Hunt asked me if you'd like one of the pups his kelpie's just had,' his mother said, drying the rest of her tear-smeared face with the tea towel.

Eric shook his head. 'No, I don't want one,' he said, because he knew quite suddenly that his life of gratitude to Mr Hunt was now over. His life would be different now.

'I didn't know what else to do, Eric,' his mother said again.

'It's nothing,' he said. 'I just didn't want that pony any more.'

For a moment Mrs Thompson looked across the table at her quiet son, and before getting up she gave her face a last embarrassed and unnecessary wipe with the cloth, and she said gently, 'You're a good boy, Eric.'

And Eric felt again that something had changed in his life, and more than ever now he was impatient to get back to normal.

What took time was his ability to get himself the two miles to school. Mrs Thompson had brought him books from Dora Hunt and from Father O'Connel and from his teacher, Miss Singleton, and though he had read all the books twice, he knew that his return to normality would only begin when he was back at school.

He managed it after six weeks, and as he made his way along the familiar street, swinging on one crutch like an expert, he was greeted first by Mrs Halford in her garden. She left off her autumn digging and clipping and came to the fence when Eric said, 'Hello, Mrs Halford.'

'Hello, Eric,' she said. 'How's your leg?'

'A bit soft,' he said. 'I mean stiff. But I'll be off my crutch in another week.'

'That was bad luck, though, wasn't it,' she said. 'Falling off like that.'

'I didn't fall off,' he said. 'The pony threw me off.' He swung around on his crutch then and said, 'Goodbye, Mrs Halford,' as he went on his way.

'Goodbye, Eric,' she said and called after him, 'Come and tell us all the gory details next time.'

He waved his hand because this time he had left Mrs Halford who would say that night to her son, Bob, 'That boy's changed.' To which Bob would reply, 'So would you if you'd been knocked on the head.' To which his mother would answer, 'No, it's not that. You'll see . . .'

Eric progressed step by step by the old route he had always taken before he had owned the pony, and it was more or less the same thing with everybody else he met, except Father O'Connel whom he saw riding a bicycle near the Catholic

School. Eric waved and stopped and waited for the priest to throw his leg over the seat and get off.

'Well I'll be damned,' Father O'Connel said. 'How are you, Snow?'

'All right, Father,' Eric said.

'What about your horse? I hear Bert Hunt's got him.'

'Yes. But he's all right.'

'How do you feel about that?'

'I don't mind,' Eric said.

'Yes, you do,' Father O'Connel said. 'But your mother was right.' And he sighed heavily and said: 'Never mind, Snow. Some day you'll be rich and famous and you can buy a horse of your own.'

Eric knew that Father O'Connel was trying to cheer him up with his old teasing game, but Eric didn't say anything because he knew that he would never want to ride another horse.

'You'll get over it,' Father O'Connel said.

'Yes, I suppose so,' Eric said boldly.

Father O'Connel put a finger in his ear, an old mode of thought for the priest, and then he ruffled Eric's white hair in a rare gesture and flung his leg over his bicycle and rode on into the Catholic school grounds.

At school, when he was greeted by verbal slaps on the back and by a lot of teasing about his broom crutch and his stiff left leg and his quick skill in manoeuvering himself on his one crutch, Eric was not surprised when none of the boys mentioned the pony. It seemed normal to them as it was to him that he should lose it, and they seemed to know that in losing it he was no longer the same boy. But it was Eric who was happy among them, and it was he who enjoyed the jokes and the teasing, and it was he who left off any conversation when he wanted to. And when Smiley called out to him, 'Old hoppy Thompson ... you just wait ... I'll get you tomorrow!' he didn't mind because he knew they were all his friends.

In class even Miss Singleton, his teacher, made a point of talking to him. 'Well, Eric, you're back from the wars. How long will you be a wounded soldier?'

'Only another week, Miss Singleton.'

'You'll have a lot to catch up in class.'

'I'll catch up,' he said. 'Don't worry.'

Miss Singleton looked at Eric, and she too saw something she had not seen before in this curious boy who lived in that tiny house with his tiny mother and who looked out at the world with bright green eyes. 'I'm sure you will,' she said, and she knew that she meant it.

Finally there was Dora Hunt, who said to him as they met briefly after school, 'It must have been awful – I mean what happened to you.'

'I didn't feel it much,' he said.

'Brownie is perfectly all right,' she said. 'He wasn't that badly hurt, and my father says you can come and ride him any time you like.'

'I don't want to ride him any more,' he said. 'He's yours now, isn't he?'

'Yes. Your mother made us take him. I wouldn't have taken him otherwise. She begged us to.'

'I know . . .'

'I've been riding him almost every day. He's so lovely, Eric.'

'Don't forget to watch his ears,' he told her. 'When he flattens them down he suddenly turns his head and tries to bite your leg.'

'He hasn't done it yet,' she said.

'Well just watch out, that's all.'

And as they parted Eric felt no rancour or resentment for Dora. She was a girl, that was all. On the Saturday he returned to Mr Hunt's store to weigh Slash's potatoes, and Slash offered him six weeks' money even though Slash himself had been forced to dirty his apron and weigh his own potatoes.

'No thanks, Slash,' Eric said. 'But thanks for the crutches.'

He had expected to see Mr Hunt, but Mr Hunt was away at one of his other stores in Nooah, and Eric was glad because he knew that he was finished with Mr Hunt. He was a kind man, and Eric liked him and decided that he would some day be as generous as Mr Hunt. But he also knew that kindness was not enough, and he was glad that his mother had paid her debt to Mr Hunt with the pony. Now they were even.

When he had finished Slash's potatoes and was leaving the back way along the lane he met Dora on the pony. She was dressed in jodhpurs, and she was on a new saddle and the pony shone beautifully and was polite and quiet. As they met face to face Eric unconsciously rubbed the pony's nose, but as if to emphasize his change in loyalties the pony pulled away.

'You behave, Brownie!' Dora said to the pony without getting off.

In fact that was what the pony was doing so well – behaving: and in his own way Eric was glad that Dora had him. If that was the way the pony wanted to be, all right that was what he wanted to be. And it was what his mother wanted. Dora would look after him, and he would probably look after her.

As he left them he made one of his secret half-whistling noises of affection which had always made the pony turn his head and come running to him. But the pony ignored him, and as Eric swung himself home on his broomstick he knew for sure that if he had never used a saddle, never seen it or touched it, ever, and then ridden that day behind the Taffies without a saddle, Red Indian style, the pony would never have tried to throw him, and the two of them would have enjoyed that wild and stormy ride. Above all, the pony would not have been frightened and they would have been Red Indians together and lost themselves once more in the tantalizing emptiness all round them.

But he also knew that he wasn't a Red Indian any more

because, in the end, he would have to be something better than that. And if he had lost one real friend of his own he would soon find another, although he doubted if he would ever find one as close and as beautiful and as trusting and as loyal as that nameless and rebellious pony, now called Brownie.

Heard about the Puffin Club?

... it's a way of finding out more about Puffin books and authors, of winning prizes (in competitions), sharing jokes, a secret code, and perhaps seeing your name in print! When you join you get a copy of our magazine, *Puffin Post*, sent to you four times a year, a badge and a membership book.
For details of subscription and an application form, send a stamped addressed envelope to:

The Puffin Club Dept A
Penguin Books Limited
Bath Road
Harmondsworth
Middlesex UB7 ODA

and if you live in Australia, please write to:

The Australian Puffin Club
Penguin Books Australia Limited
P.O. Box 257
Ringwood
Victoria 3134